The author is currently a teacher of English language and has a degree in Humanities with Literature. She enjoys reading 19th-century fiction, in particular Charles Dickens and Thomas Hardy.

Having grown up in Devon, Alison Huntingford has always had a strong affinity to the county, despite being born elsewhere. One of her favourite pastimes is genealogy and she was therefore delighted to find an ancestor who came from Exeter in Devon. His story inspired her recent novel, *The Glass Bulldog*.

In her spare time, she enjoys spending time with her husband and their pets, listening to music, going to the cinema and gardening.

Dedicated to my wonderful husband, Nigel, for believing in me; my mother, Kathleen, for always being there; and Maisie Smith, for help and inspiration.

Best wishes.
Alison Huntingford x

DISCLAIMER

Although this book is a work of fiction, much of it is based on documented historical fact. Did the events described within actually happen? I do not know. I merely suggest that they could have happened.

Alison Huntingford

THE GLASS BULLDOG

AUSTIN MACAULEY PUBLISHERS™

LONDON · CAMBRIDGE · NEW YORK · SHARJAH

A CIP catalogue record for this title is available from the British Library.

ISBN 9781528914161 (Paperback)
ISBN 9781528960809 (ePub e-book)

www.austinmacauley.com

First Published (2019)
Austin Macauley Publishers Ltd
25 Canada Square
Canary Wharf
London
E14 5LQ

Thanks to:
Rowena Jay   Alphington Miscellany and Memories
The Alphington Archives www.alphington.org.uk
Mavis Saunters, descendant of Molly and James Cooper
Ancestry.co.uk
FindMyPast.co.uk
Genes Reunited
London Metropolitan Police website
Wikipedia
Devon Records Office
GRO

Prologue

The glass bulldog sits on the shelf in the bedroom, the sunlight glinting off the smoked glass. It is chipped and worn with age, fragile yet still strong. Many years have passed since it was first created and someone might wonder what stories it could tell. What memories does it hold? We can only guess.

Chapter 1
Alphington, Exeter, 1833

Tom smiled. It was a while since this had happened, as he hadn't had much to smile about recently. However, the approach of the lovely Mary Ann always made him smile. They were both very young (Tom was 16 years old), but he thought he would probably marry her one day. Her long, fair hair was the colour of warm honey, and as it moved gently in the breeze, Tom wished this image could stay with him forever. Though she was only 15 years old, she had the makings of a beautiful woman in the future. At present, she had a sweetness and an innocent charm which made him want to cherish and protect her against the evils of the world.

Of the world he knew little as yet, but he had certainly seen some distressing things so far. Only last year there had been the dreaded cholera outbreak and he shuddered to think back.

Tom's family were farming folk. Not that they were wealthy enough to own a farm, no, but they worked for a farmer as labourers, helping with the crops, planting, harvesting, sowing, reaping. The farm animals also needed their daily care. Tom's Father, Richard Finnimore, had always worked for Farmer Lapthorne and had been treated strictly but fairly. The hours were long and the work hard, but the family had survived on what he received in pay. Now that the older boys (John, Will, Dick and Tom) were old enough to work they were bringing in some more as well, so the large family of eight children had been doing okay. Not rich, but getting by.

Alphington was a pleasant rural village in Devon, quite bustling at times with regular stage coaches passing through. Consequently, there were many stables, blacksmiths, saddlers and other associated trades to serve the coaches and their passengers. Nonetheless, it still retained its own identity, quite separate from the nearby city of Exeter, with a community mostly of farming folk due to having a great deal of fertile land. There was a local squire and some other landowners who often traded in horses at the annual fair or sold cattle at the local market, but most of the villagers were agricultural labourers, many living in tied cottages. There were a handful of shops and other businesses, some alehouses and an attempt at a local school. The local gentry were of a reasonably generous disposition and provision was often made for the poor. For example, in the year Tom was born (1816), at Christmas all the poor received gifts of meat to feed their families. The church also provided entertainment such as dances, concerts and a Sunday school. Reverend Ellicombe, the son of the previous vicar, was a good man who worked hard. All in all, it wasn't a bad place to live.

That was until last year, when everything changed due to the cholera. It had started when a visitor arrived in nearby St Thomas and died soon afterwards. In spite of the best efforts of the medics and the authorities, the poor water quality spread the disease like wildfire around the neighbouring villages. Alphington, where Tom and his family lived, was very near to this area and soon had its share of victims. It spread through the water system as fast as a bad rumour. The very leats that were so valuable to everyone's lives became the poison that killed them in their dozens.

It was a hot summer day in early August, when Tom's little sister Annie, only six years old, became ill. She had been out playing by the leat with her friends only a few days before.

"Tom!" called his mother, Sarah. "Run down and fetch the Doctor. Our Annie's not well!"

Tom came running in from the yard where he had been feeding the chickens. (He only worked part time at present, so he helped out around the home as well).

Annie was the favourite out of his siblings. She had a gentle sensitivity and quiet nature that he loved. Like most of their family (himself included), she had dark wavy hair and deep velvety brown eyes. Although she was only six, she was wise beyond her years. She appeared to have a natural inclination to see the divine in everything. Only the other day she asked him why God created rainbows. Perplexed, Tom could only reply that he guessed the Almighty liked the colours. She made him think about things that had never occurred to him before. Tom had had very little education, though there was a small school in the village which he attended for a short while. There was one master, Mr Marker, who did his best to teach some of the poor boys of the parish. (Girls were not admitted). Here Tom had learnt to read and to name plants and animals. Despite this, he had never been taught writing and could not sign his own name. The lessons were mostly based around practical subjects with a hearty dose of religious morals thrown in for good measure. The pupils were brought up to be useful, polite, well-behaved citizens.

Now he went into the front room to see Annie lying wrapped up in blankets by the fire. Her forehead was damp with sweat. Earlier that day she'd started being sick all the time and now she was so weak she could hardly focus on Tom's face. Their mother had heard the rumours of the dreadful disease that was sweeping through Exeter and now she feared the worst.

"Annie," whispered Tom. "It's alright. I'll get the Doctor. You'll feel better soon."

He held her hand but she barely noticed. He kissed her gently on the forehead then sped off to get the local physician, Mr Calder. This was easier said than done however, as when Tom got to his house, he found the medic was out already, tending other sick villagers. His wife suggested the local curate who was also helping out. The village of Alphington was small, but the roads were quite winding and it took Tom several minutes to get to the curate's humble lodgings near St Michael's Church. He banged on the door for all he was worth. The curate, Mr Cooper, came hastily to the door.

"Please help us!" cried Tom. "My little sister is awful poorly and needs your help!"

Mr Cooper grabbed his bag and followed Tom back to their small farm cottage. On the way, the curate told Tom how widespread the disease was around Exeter. Every day dozens more were falling ill, with many fatalities. Sometimes it was only a matter of hours. Treatment was limited and quite primitive.

"Only yesterday," said the curate, "I went to a house in St Thomas, where both the husband and wife died the same day. Pity the little children left behind – may God have mercy on them."

Tom shuddered.

When they reached their humble cottage, Tom's mother was watching anxiously from the doorway. Annie was worse, having dreadful pain from muscle cramps and not able to keep anything down, even water. Her skin had become a bluish grey all over. The curate gave her tinctures of rhubarb as a purgative and let some blood, but neither seemed to give her much relief. To be fair to the curate, he had no medical training and had just been advised what to do by the local physician, as everyone was so run off their feet with new cases appearing every hour. The curate left and Tom went down to the local shop with his younger sister Lizzie to get some provisions. When they got there, however, the shopkeeper, Mr Lethbridge, in contrast to his usual jovial manner, refused to let them in.

"We don't want none of your disease 'round here, boy! We've heard you got the plague. Go away!"

"That's not fair!" cried Lizzie. "*We're* not ill and we need the food!"

She was almost in tears, but Tom understood. He always tried to see the other person's point of view. People were frightened and with good reason.

"Look, mister," he reasoned. "Can't we work something out? Annie's real sick and Ma is desperate."

"Well, okay," said the shopkeeper, softening a bit. "Leave your money outside the door and I'll slide the food through the winder to you. What do you need?"

So that's what they did, but everywhere they went it was the same. People were scared and didn't want to get involved with anyone else's problems in case they caught it too. They hurried away as soon as they saw them. Normally people greeted you and stopped to chat. The cholera had changed all that. Now it was every man for himself. There was an air of mistrust and paranoia in the village that had never been there before.

On the way home, however, they ran into John Martin, Tom's best mate. John was a bit of a fiery redhead, but was fun to be around. He was lively and inventive, and often led the quieter and more reticent Tom into misadventures. When their families both attended church on Sunday, John had kept Tom laughing with his impressions of the minister, and then got them both into further trouble by carving rude figures on the sides of the pews! The sexton thought it was both of them and came 'round with his cane. Only Tom's mother had managed to stop them both getting a beating.

Seeing Tom and Lizzie now he came running down to talk to them.

"Tom! Lizzie! Have you heard the news about that awful disease? Ma and Pa have both got it, and Susan too! There's only me left that's well. I don't know what to do!"

Tom sympathised and told him about Annie. When Lizzie related the story of the shopkeeper's behaviour, John was shocked and furious.

"How can they be like that? Don't they know we're suffering and people are dying? Surely people can help each other!"

They parted soon afterwards as John was off to try and find the doctor or anyone else who could help. Tom promised him they would always help out if they could. He had been brought up believing that you should never turn anyone away who was in trouble. When they got back home, however, they found that little Annie had had a seizure and was now lying pale, cold and still as death. The curate had told them that this was the second stage of the cholera and that the patient must be kept warm with friction, blankets, warm fires etc. to try and pass through this stage. Tom worked tirelessly, chopping and bringing in wood to keep the fire going and the room warm. His mother rubbed Annie's limbs with towels to heat her up. Lizzie prepared meals and drinks for everyone in their mother's place. In spite of all this, it was to no avail as Annie was sinking fast, and by the early hours of the next morning she had passed away.

Sadly for Tom, he didn't get to say a final goodbye to Annie. She never regained consciousness that evening and when the moment actually came, poor Tom was outside collecting more logs. There was no sad farewell or lingering kiss, just a gurgle, a splutter and Annie was gone. He came back in with an armful of logs to find his mother crying and his father trying not to. The younger children were in bed but Tom's older brothers, Will, Dick and John, stood around helplessly. Dick put his arms around their mother who was distraught. Their father just sat there with his head in his hands, numb with pain. Tom couldn't take it in. It seemed so sudden it was unreal. Surely it was just a bad dream. He couldn't cry, in fact he felt a hysterical laugh rising in his throat, but he managed to choke it down. He felt guilty that he couldn't cry. He knew it couldn't be right, but somehow the tears wouldn't come. Ever practical, he busied himself with the fire and making tea for everyone. It helped to keep busy. Somehow this had to be got through.

His father wrapped Annie's body in a sheet and suggested they all go to bed. They didn't know what else to do. Tom thought he would never sleep but when he got to bed he was so exhausted that sleep just overwhelmed him. With it, however, came troubling dreams and he awoke feeling just as tired as before.

The next morning brought yet more troubles and grief of a different kind. Tom's father and older brothers went off to work in the fields at 7 am as usual, leaving Tom to look after his mother and younger siblings. Tom was given the unenviable task of going down to fetch the vicar to discuss the details of Annie's burial. Reverend Ellicombe, a middle-aged man who had baptised all the children of the family, was sad to hear the news. He came along with Tom to their cottage to talk to his mother. As they returned, however, Tom could see a group of people gathered outside their house. The front door was open and a commotion was going on inside. His mother was shouting and screaming. The younger children, Ed, Lizzie and Sarah, were huddled around her, crying. There seemed to be lots of people in their home, some of whom wore uniforms and all of whom seemed to be engaged in emptying the house of its meagre contents. Tom rushed in to see what was happening. He was horrified to see some men removing Annie's body along with all of her clothes, toys and belongings.

"What's going on?" he demanded. "Leave her alone!"

"Sorry, lad. All infected bodies and materials have to be removed. It's an order of government. She'll be buried in St Bartholomew's Yard in Exeter. That's where all the pox cases go."

"Leave her things alone," begged his mother tearfully. "She loved those toys and that's her best Sunday dress!"

"Sorry, ma'am, these all have to be burnt, in case of spreading the infection."

"No!" his mother cried. "Please!" But the men wouldn't listen. All Annie's favourite things were bagged up and taken away. Her body was lifted onto a cart.

Tom rushed after them. "When will she be buried? Please tell us. We want to have someone say some words for her."

"It'll be two o' clock this Wednesday, lad. St Bartholomew's Yard, Exeter, along with all the others."

The vicar managed to find out a few more details from the men before they finally took her away. Meanwhile, other men emptied their entire house out on to the pavement and then lime-washed all the walls and ceilings inside. Despite their protests, all their bedding was bagged up and taken away for burning. A collection of rough, hard blankets and sheets was given to them to replace it.

"Sorry, lady, regulations!" said one of the men to his mother. "Can't be helped. It's for your own good, you know!"

The local neighbours watched it all, which Tom found humiliating. His family were poor but they still had their pride.

"What you staring at?" he cried. They turned away embarrassed, but no one stopped to offer comfort or help.

Hours later, Tom and his family had finally managed to put all the furniture back in place and remake the beds. His father and brothers came back from the fields hungry, but could only have bread and cheese as no one had had time to prepare any food. It was a miserable day.

Wednesday came at last, but offered little relief. Tom and his family made their way sadly to Bartholomew's yard. They were shocked, however, to see the amount of burials all going on at the same time. Each burial pit was eight feet deep to prevent future infection. The coffin and everything around it was sprinkled with quick lime as well. However, the worst thing was the crowd. A large, angry mob had gathered and was shouting at the graveyard workers trying to do their job. It appeared, from Tom's understanding, that it consisted of locals terrified of infection from the bodies. Tom stayed close to his family, until suddenly he saw his friend, John Martin, across the yard. He hurried across to speak to him. John was angry and distraught. He told Tom he had lost his whole family.

"I've nothing left!" he said bitterly. "Nothing! How could this awful disease do this? What is wrong with the world? Why will no one help?"

Tom tried his best to console him, but John's face was set like stone, angry and hard. His friend would never be the same. He had lost too much. Tom also heard that John was likely to lose his home as it was a tied cottage linked to his father's work and the farmer now wanted him out.

It was now nearly two o' clock, so Tom hurried back to his family. As the vicar tried to say some words over Annie, the mob started to draw nearer, shouting at them, throwing stones and threatening them.

"Get outta here! We don't want your evil sickness! Clear off!"

Some of Tom's older brothers took it into their heads to start arguing back, especially when his mother and sisters started crying. In no time at all, punches started to fly and the funeral became a brawl. It was an awful episode. Tom tried his best to shelter his mum from the missiles flying all around them. Although he was angry at the injustice of it all, he had no inclination to fight; he just wanted to protect his family. The other burials seemed to be having similar problems and the graveyard, instead of being a place of peaceful grieving, became a battleground. Eventually, the riot was broken up by the local officials and Tom and his family retreated sadly. The vicar managed to say a few brief words over Annie's grave, but no one felt that they had had a proper chance to say goodbye. They left the graveyard feeling worse than when they came. The older brothers were bruised, his mother and sisters very shaken and Tom felt unfulfilled and dissatisfied. A proper funeral allowed people to accept the death and move on, but this certainly hadn't achieved this. It would be many years before Tom finally got over it.

Chapter 2

It was a couple of months later and Tom had recently met Mary Ann at the annual horse fair in Alphington. This was held at Michaelmas every year and was, he had heard, the biggest in Devon. It lasted two days. It was a large and riotous event with gypsies trading horses and many hostelries open for the occasion. This year, there were as many as twenty public houses open and the locals took every opportunity to indulge, Tom included. The scene at the fair was noisy and colourful. Everywhere you looked there were horses and people. Besides this there were side stalls selling all manner of goods as well as fairground rides, music and singing, dog shows, competitions and fortune telling booths. Tom's whole family were attending this year and his mother insisted on them all going home to a cooked goose at the end of the day. As the saying went: '*Eat a goose on Michaelmas Day, want not for money all the year!*' Certainly they could do with some more money at the moment, as times were hard locally after the cholera outbreak. The farmer had had to lay off workers, including his father, and now his brothers were having to find work as tanners instead of farm labourers. His father was struggling to find new work and many people locally had had to take pay cuts. Tom was under pressure to join his brothers, but he really didn't want to. He loved to grow things. Feeling the soil on his hands and seeing the first shoots come up was so rewarding. At present he was looking after the chickens at home and growing vegetables for the family, but he knew this couldn't last. He'd been working part time on the farm since the age of 12 until they were all laid off, and he needed to earn a living. He reflected that it was sad that doing things you loved didn't pay the bills unfortunately. He didn't know much about the tanning industry, but what he had heard so far certainly didn't recommend itself to him.

Today, by contrast, everyone was out to enjoy themselves and forget the sad memories of recent times. Tom wandered happily through the fair with his sister Lizzie, trying out the various amusements, until he spied his old friend, John Martin approaching with an attractive young lady on his arm. Their eyes met immediately and Tom felt himself blushing. John introduced the fair young lady as his cousin, Mary Ann Portbury. Tom gazed at her in awe, not sure what to say. He noticed everything about her, from the way her hair gently curled around the nape of her neck to the curves of her dress. She had the figure of a woman but still the innocence of a young girl. John suggested Tom and Lizzie join them and any awkwardness was quickly forgotten. Tom shyly suggested that Mary Ann could not possibly be related to a rogue like John and she laughed. Her laugh was like silver, sparkling water rushing over pebbles in a stream. Tom thought he had never heard anything more beautiful. The four of them wandered around the fair together, Lizzie mostly spending time chatting to John, who, it must be admitted, she had a bit of a crush on. Tom and Mary Ann chatted, laughed and generally got to know each other. There was an immediate connection. It seemed like they knew all about each other already, almost as if they'd known each other all their lives. By the end of that day, they were inseparable. When Tom and Lizzie went back to their home for the roast goose at the end of the day, John and Mary Ann went with them and a merry time was had by all. It was the first time everyone had seemed happy since the awful day of the funeral.

As the months went by, Tom and Mary Ann spent more time together, walking in the countryside, spending time with each other's families and occasionally going to local dances. They both loved music and nature, so they had a lot in common. Mary Ann was an innocent, simple, country girl who seemed untouched by recent local events. However, she was lively, quick-witted and saw the funny side of everything. She made Tom laugh in a way he hadn't in many months. John was now living at her family home, having lost all his own family. Tom was a bit jealous at first, worried that John may get close to Mary Ann, but it seemed they had nothing in common. John's impulsiveness and increasing bitterness was fast turning people away from him. Tom understood his friend's anger and sadness, but had learnt to accept his own loss and move on. He did his best to support him, but John was increasingly getting into scrapes and fights. He drank too much and showed little inclination to earn a living. Mary Ann's father kept trying to find openings for him but John kept failing to turn up when he was supposed to, or was slapdash in his work. Finally, Mr Portbury snapped and said either John stuck at the next job he got him, or move out and find his own way in the world.

Meanwhile, Tom had reached his sixteenth birthday and was horrified to find his brother, Richard, had secured a job for him at the local tanning yard. Tom knew he would have to take the job. Since the cholera outbreak, his father and older brothers couldn't get any more work at the farm, as the farmer had lost most of his own family and was considering giving up. He could no longer afford to employ extra workers. Tom's mother was frequently complaining that the money no longer made ends meet and food was becoming harder to come by. Prices had gone up, wages had gone down and times were hard. The family were often hungry now. Sometimes there was only bread and milk for supper. The sad day came when even the chickens had to be eaten as they were running so short of food. Tom felt bad as he had enjoyed looking after them.

Tom discovered first hand that tanning was disgusting work. First, the fresh animal skins would be soaked in water with lime or urine added to burn off the hair. The smell was dreadful and the lime solution dangerous and caustic to the skin. Tom saw one worker with dreadful scars on his face as a result of it splashing up when fresh skins were dropped in. The man had been lucky not to lose his sight. After soaking the skins, they then had to be scraped and pounded to remove all the flesh and hair. This was Tom's job. After the first week, his hands were red, raw and bleeding.

Once this awful process was finished, then dog faeces or other animal dung was kneaded into it to soften it. This could take two or three hours. Finally the hides were soaked again in water with added tannin from tree bark to clean it and harden it. The whole procedure took a long time. Tom decided the tanning process was like a journey through hell.

No matter how hard he tried, Tom could not remove the ghastly smell from his clothes, hair and body. Mary Ann reeled when he first saw her at the end of that week. She refused to go near him as he smelt so bad. Tom had been desperately waiting to see her all week and had scrubbed himself down thoroughly. He hoped it would be okay. When he went around to Mary Ann's house to take her to the local dance, he went to embrace her as usual but was soundly rejected.

"Ughhh!" cried Mary Ann. "What's that dreadful smell? It's awful!"

"Oh, Mary Ann," said Tom. "I can't help it. I've worked hard all week. Come and kiss me."

But she pushed him away when he tried saying, "Don't come near me!"

He was surprised to find her so intolerant. He had thought she would be more understanding.

"Look at your hands!" she said. "They're bleeding. Don't touch me. I can't bear it!"

"It's not my fault," begged Tom. "Please, Mary Ann, don't be like that!"

It was their first row. Tom felt hurt by her attitude, although he agreed with her opinion of the smell. He had only managed to put up with the work and the stench all week by imagining he could save up enough money to ask her to be his wife. Now these dreams seemed dashed. *What future do we have now?* he thought. *How can I ask her to marry me? She will never put up with me like this.*

Tom tried to persuade Mary Ann to still come to the dance but she flatly refused and shut the door on him, saying, "I'm sorry, Tom, but you need to do something else for a job if you want to take me out. How could you do this to me? Even a thief wouldn't smell as bad as you!"

Tom was depressed. He spoke to his mother about the argument and told her how upset he was, but his mother seemed to think it would all blow over.

"I'm sorry you have to do a job you hate, Tom," she said. "But that's life! We have to survive. You know how tight things are now. I'd really like to say, 'leave and do something else', but it's not that easy. There's not much work around now and at least the pay for tanning is not too bad. The family needs your help, Tom. You know we are struggling, and I don't know where the next meal is coming from, really I don't! I'm sure she'll come 'round when she's thought about it. I'm sorry, but we really need you to help bring some food in for us all."

His mother looked tired, worried and a bit tearful and Tom gave her a hug, but he didn't really agree with what she said. When his father came home, though, Tom noticed how anxious he looked and how he went without supper so that the little ones could eat.

Not knowing which way to turn, he arranged to meet up with his friend John for a drink the next night. Tom felt hurt and sad. Together they bemoaned their lot and tried to think of ways to improve their lives. Earlier that day, John had yet again got into trouble with the farmer he was working for when he accidentally let the cows loose by forgetting to fasten the field gate. He knew he was going to get sacked again and that this meant the end of staying at his Uncle's house. John was angry and desperate.

That evening, Tom and John had far too much to drink. Their voices got louder and angrier and the schemes they dreamt up got wilder as the night wore on. At one point they were going to run away to sea, at another they were going to dig for gold! None of it was very serious. Eventually, the alehouse closed for the night and the two young men reluctantly left, shouting and staggering as they went up the road.

"I know!" shouted John drunkenly. "Let's go and see Farmer Spart! He's got some fine chickens that would make a meal or two. That would help your mum out, wouldn't it, Tom? Mary Ann and her family can't fail to be impressed by a good chicken dinner. The bastard owes me for all the work I've done for him this week anyway!"

Tom was in no fit state to reason or argue. He was an angry drunk prepared to do anything. In a drunken haze he remembered his mother's strained and worried face. Maybe he could make her happy again? She wanted him to feed the family, maybe this was a way to help? Perhaps Mary Ann would love him again if he could do something other than tanning? He remembered vaguely that she had said she would prefer a thief to a tanner. It all made some kind of strange sense at the time.

The two of them staggered down the lane and through the farmyard to where the chickens were kept. Unfortunately, they were making quite a lot of noise, unaware that they were being watched. They reached the henhouse and John entered grabbing several fowls which he passed to Tom. They were clucking loudly and struggling. Tom could hardly hold them and started to laugh wildly himself. It all seemed a big joke, another one of John's pranks.

John went back into the coop again, but as he came out this time clutching some more chickens, a voice cried, "Stay there, thieves, or I'll shoot!"

The farmer stood there, eyes blazing, a shot gun in his hands. With all the noise they had been making, neither of them had heard him approach.

"John Martin – I might have guessed!" he exclaimed. "But Tom Finnimore – I thought you knew better. Wait till I see your families. Drop those chickens immediately!"

There was nothing they could do. They returned the chickens to the henhouse and reluctantly went with the farmer. As he had a gun, they did not have much choice. Farmer Spart was a hard-hearted man and their drunken pleas for mercy and profuse apologies had no effect on him. He immediately called the local constable, and by the early morning hours they had been marched off to the local holding gaol. This was a tiny round house, barely big enough for the two of them, let alone the other three people incarcerated there. It was not a place that anyone would want to linger in.

Chapter 3

Tom woke up the following morning in a haze. His head ached and he felt sick to his stomach. When he first came 'round, he couldn't remember where he was or what had happened. Then it all suddenly came back to him in a horrifying rush – the drinking, the shouting, the taking of the chickens. Why had he been such a fool? It wasn't like him normally. He remembered the argument with Mary Ann and knew in his heart of hearts that it was mostly because of this. He felt ashamed and embarrassed as he remembered Constable Strawbridge (who was only a volunteer after all) having to be woken from his bed at two in the morning to collect them and take them to this hell hole of a gaol. He also remembered Farmer Spart's angry face, red with rage at their offence. Tom knew the farmer would never let this drop. He wasn't known to be forgiving. He was bad tempered at any time and a harsh master. People didn't cross him if they could help it.

After a basic breakfast of bread and water, he and John were taken before the local magistrate, Sir William Nation. Being a local landowner himself, he was severe on them both and indicted them both for six counts of theft, one for each chicken. Tom tried desperately to apologise and explain it was a moment of drunken madness, but John's defiant and angry attitude did nothing to help their case. They were committed and ordered to appear before the Magistrates Court in Exeter, at the next quarter session, at Epiphany. The court would meet on New Year's Eve.

'Great!' thought Tom bitterly. 'That's a brilliant start to 1834.'

In the meantime, they were offered bail and allowed to go home as long as they kept in touch with the local constable. John, however, no longer had a home to go to as Mary Ann's father would now certainly throw him out. Therefore he was ordered to stay in the local gaol, at which he protested vehemently but to no avail. Tom's father had been sent for and under his custody, Tom was allowed to leave.

His father said little when he first collected him and escorted him home, but once home, he berated Tom loudly in front of the whole family.

"How could you do this?" he cried. "You've brought shame to us all! We're a hard-working, honest family. Couldn't you have been more sensible?"

Tom's mother was in tears, which affected Tom even more than the telling off from his father. His brothers could hardly look him in the eye and Lizzie just gazed sadly at him.

The time leading up to Christmas from that November was a terrible one for Tom. He was drowning in misery. He had lost his job at the tanning yard and so had to help around the house again. He didn't mind the work, but the shame was a lot to bear. Neighbours tried to ignore him and old friends passed him by. However, one day, towards the end of November, he had an unexpected visitor. He opened the door and Mary Ann stood there, looking uncertain and a bit tearful.

"Tom," she began. "I'm so sorry. This is all my fault!"

Tom didn't know what to say so he just took her in his arms and kissed her. Everything was suddenly okay between them again. All the harsh words were forgotten.

"I wanted to come before," said Mary Ann, when she had breath to speak, "but my father was so angry he wouldn't let me. He won't even hear John's name mentioned in the house."

Tom felt bad when he remembered his friend stuck in jail all this time, but he reflected that he would also be ending up there soon.

Mary Ann continued, "Father's calmed down a bit now, after I told him about our row and how I felt it was my fault. He agreed that I could see you just once. What do you think they will do to you?"

Tom wasn't sure. He had heard tales of punishments like the stocks, the treadmill, transportation or imprisonment on the 'hulks'. The hulks were out of service military ships, moored just off the coast, used as makeshift prisons. Word was that conditions were awful and disease was rife. Tom dreaded the idea of these.

Worse still, however, was the thought that he might even be hung. In Alphington there was a local gallows at the square, which was still used, though, thankfully, not as often as it used to be. In older times, people would be hung just for stealing sheep, but nowadays it was usually reserved for more serious crimes like murder. At least Tom hoped as much. His heart filled with horror at the thought of it.

Tom and Mary Ann's reconciliation was sweet but brief. She promised to wait for him no matter what, but Tom knew he might never return home again after the trial.

"Look, Mary Ann," he said sadly. "I wanted to ask you to be my wife but I've no right to ask it now. It may be a long time till I'm free. We've got to face the truth. You must find another man whose future is brighter than mine. Just remember me as a man who really loved you."

They embraced, but Mary Ann left in tears and Tom was close to them himself. He had loved Mary Ann more than anyone or anything, but everything was ruined now by one act of drunken stupidity. He was in despair.

Tom didn't know anything about how the courts worked. He was scared and thought maybe it would help to talk to someone more learned than him. He thought of the school master, Mr Marker, but he had never got on that well with him. The teacher appeared to be a stern, cold-hearted sort of man. Maybe appearances could be deceptive, but Tom didn't feel he could talk to him. The other option was the local clergy. Reverend Ellicombe was a gentle, caring man who had done much to help the villagers in the cholera outbreak and appeared to be understanding. So after church one Sunday Tom grabbed him as he came out and pleaded to have a few words with him. The Reverend agreed and they went back to the parsonage to talk. Reverend Ellicombe was a middle-aged man now, with grey hair and whiskers. He took Tom into the parlour of the vicarage and offered him tea. The parlour was warm and cosy with high backed leather armchairs and a roaring log fire. Tom felt comfortable there and wished his own home could be more like it. Their cottage had bare whitewashed walls and plain wooden floorboards, with a couple of rugs. Their furniture was basic and rough, but still it was home all the same.

Tom started hesitantly, but to his relief the vicar had already heard of his plight, so Tom had no need to explain.

"I know all about it, my son," he said kindly. "So take your time. You are not being judged here."

Tom breathed a sigh of relief. "Well," he said. "I wondered if you knew anything about what happens when you go to court. I'm so worried. I don't know what I am supposed to do or say. You being a much more learned man, I hoped you might know."

The vicar smiled. "I've never been in your unfortunate position, Tom," he replied, "but I do know something of the procedures. The first thing you ought to know is that the worst thing you can possibly do is to plead guilty, because they will give you the maximum sentence they can!"

"But I am guilty!" cried Tom. "How can I say I'm not?"

"Well," said the vicar thoughtfully, "that's true, but maybe you could say there are 'mitigating circumstances'."

"You what?" asked Tom. He had never heard of this term before.

"Reasons why you did what you did," explained the vicar.

"Oh, I see," said Tom and proceeded to tell him all about the row, his family's hardship, his mixed up emotions and the drinking.

The vicar listened carefully and sympathised. "All I can say, Tom, is that you could say 'not guilty by reason of drunkenness.' In other words, you weren't in your right mind. It probably won't get you off, but it may help reduce the sentence."

He then proceeded to tell Tom as much as he knew about the trials. The victim of the crime (in this case Farmer Spart) was usually the prosecutor and would put their case to the judge. The accused (Tom) would then have to answer the charges. They were always presumed guilty first and had to try and prove their innocence. They could have a person speak for their character but otherwise they were on their own. There were multiple cases tried in a day, often as many as 15 to 20. The jury were then instructed to make decisions on them as quickly as possible. As the jury was kept without food, drink or warmth until they agreed their verdicts, these were very quickly forthcoming. After all, no one wanted to sit around for hours, uncomfortable and hungry for the sake of a few 'criminals.' The sooner they made their decisions, the sooner they all got home. The judge then sentenced the guilty party. The judges were not known for their patience and tended to rush things through.

Tom felt depressed again. Who could speak for him? Maybe the vicar? He asked him and the vicar replied he would be happy to try, but couldn't guarantee what would happen. All the same, he agreed, which made Tom feel a bit better. Tom had always been of good character and never done anything wrong before.

Christmas came and went. It wasn't a big celebration at that time anyway for the working poor. It was just a day's holiday and a family meal if you were lucky. This year, everything felt soured. Tom knew that as soon as Christmas was over and New Year's Eve arrived he would have to appear in court to answer for his crime.

The day before New Year's Eve, Tom finally got a chance to speak to his mother about it all. Everyone else had gone to work as usual. Ever since the incident, Tom had wanted to try and talk to her about it but she had avoided the subject. The rain was pouring down outside and they were both in by the fire.

"Ma," said Tom. "I really need to talk to you about this, please. This may the last chance I get. Tomorrow I'm in court and may never get home again!"

His mother listened silently.

"I'm sorry about it all," he continued. "I really am. If I could take it all back, I would. I was so mixed up at the time, what with arguing with Mary Ann and feeling guilty I wasn't doing more to help feed the family."

She started to speak, but he raised his hand to stop her. "No Ma. Let me finish," he said. "I know it was stupid and now I'm going to pay the price. If I hadn't been drunk, I would never have done it. Please, please forgive me and at least I'll feel better in my heart." He broke down in sobs. "Ma, please!"

For answer, all his mother could do was to hold him tight, sobbing herself. When at last their tears subsided, she said, "Tom, we all love you no matter what you do, and we always will. Whatever happens, remember that!"

They hugged and then sat in companionable silence in the firelight. What the next day would bring, nobody knew.

Chapter 4

Tom awoke the next day with a sinking feeling in his stomach. He felt physically sick and faint, but he knew he had to get through this somehow. Lying in bed for a few brief precious moments he realised this might be the last time he would ever be at home. His eyes misted with tears but he blinked them away furiously. *Mustn't let my feelings get the better of me! It won't do.* He said a silent prayer to whatever 'Being' there might be to help him through the day and its results. Tom had been brought up going to church and Sunday school, but wasn't quite sure what he believed any more. Annie was a pure and gentle child, but God, or whatever He was, saw fit to take her away. This gave Tom serious doubts about heavenly justice. However, he reckoned it was worth a try and sent up a plea, just in case. Moments later, Tom was washed and dressed in his Sunday best. The Reverend said it was a good idea to look as respectable as possible in order to give a good impression. Reverend Ellicombe was going to meet Tom at the Courthouse, and would try and speak on his behalf as a character witness.

Tom tried to eat some breakfast but couldn't manage it. The food stuck in his throat, although he did manage to drink some milk. All the family gathered around him. His father was accompanying him to the trial, but the others just hugged him, wishing him well. His mother and Lizzie were silently crying. Although Tom was dreading it, it was almost a relief to finally leave the house. At least now it was underway.

His father said very little on the way, but as they checked in at the court and just before Tom got taken off to a separate waiting area, he did say, rather gruffly, "Take care, lad," and he patted him on the shoulder, which, for his father, was quite a show of emotion.

Tom knew that his father was not as emotionally tough as he looked and only got-by by not expressing how he felt. If he were to start showing it, he was scared he would lose control.

Tom was led off into a large, bare room with no seats in it, where several people were standing waiting. There he saw John Martin again, but was shocked to see him looking thin and haggard.

"John!" he cried, "How are you? I was worried about you."

"So worried that you never came to see me!" replied John bitterly. "Living it up at home and me stuck here. One rule for one and one for another, I reckon."

"Please," begged Tom. "It wasn't like that. I was only let home because I had a family to go to. It's been awful. I feel so bad for them."

"Big deal!" said John. "You don't know what it's like in jail – but you will. You wait and see. We'll both go down. You're a traitor to your friends and I'll make sure you don't get let off. You were in it as much as me!"

"I know," replied Tom. "I'm not trying to pretend that I wasn't. I'm sorry you feel like that, John."

John marched off to the other corner of the room and refused to look at or talk to him again. Tom felt desperate.

The waiting was awful and seemed to go on forever. People kept getting called in for their turn and then didn't reappear. Mostly their companions were a rough looking lot that Tom kept away from, but he did feel sorry for one elderly woman who stood there crying in a corner. Tom tried to speak to her.

"Can I help?" he asked. "What are you here for?"

She explained, between sobs, that, having been beaten and ill treated by her husband for many years, she had eventually attempted to stab him with a kitchen knife. He survived unfortunately and she was arrested. Now she was likely to face the gallows. Tom tried his best to comfort her, but couldn't think what to say.

The hours passed and having arrived at 9 am, Tom was now feeling tired and faint. There was no food or seating, only water to drink. At one time their names were called out but then delayed when someone else went in ahead of them. No one knew what was happening or when. This, apparently, was normal according to one of the rougher looking occupants of the chamber. He'd been there before for other minor crimes and didn't seem worried about it.

"It's all over in a few minutes," he explained. "They don't listen to you, whatever you say. That's just the way it is!"

Tom thought of his father and Reverend Ellicombe waiting upstairs and hoped they would be okay.

At about 3 o' clock in the afternoon, their turn finally came. Tom and John were called together. They were led up to a huge courtroom with benches around and a judge presiding. There was a jury seated at the side. The air seemed to be thick with guilt. Tom caught a brief glimpse of his father and the vicar in the gallery. Then, to his horror, he saw Farmer Spart facing them. He had no idea what he might say, as the accused were not allowed to know in advance. The theory was that if they were really innocent they would be able to prove it.

The judge gave a brief opening address, then turned the case over to Farmer Spart.

"These two rogues," started the farmer, "came to my farm on November 1st and damaged my property and stole my livestock. They smashed up my henhouse, trampled my crops and took a dozen or more live fowls for their own benefit. When I challenged them they swore and shouted at me. I was scared they were going to attack me or something. They were proper nasty!"

"How do you plead?" asked the judge.

"Not guilty!" they both cried. Tom tried to explain how things really happened and that they were drunk, but no one would listen.

"We didn't do those things," he said. "He's lying. We were drunk, but I know we didn't do all the things he says."

"If you were drunk, how would you remember?" demanded Spart.

John then spoke up, "We may have taken your chickens but that's all. We never done any of the rest!"

"Oh, so you admit it then! You see, your honour, they are guilty."

The whole trial was a muddle of lies and confusion. Tom tried to ask to bring in the Reverend as a character witness but the judge refused to consider it.

"Please," pleaded Tom. "I have someone to speak for me. I'm not a bad person. It was all a mistake."

"We don't have time to waste on unnecessary things like that. Your guilt is obvious," declared the judge. "Next!"

They had been tricked into admitting their guilt due to trying to prove themselves innocent of the things they hadn't actually done. The verdict and sentencing would be given at the end of the day. They were taken back down to another room below, depressed and silent. The whole trial had only taken 20 minutes. Tom knew they had very little hope and he wondered how the jury would remember all the details later when it came to making their decisions.

They then had a further long wait until about 7 o' clock that evening when all prisoners were recalled for their verdicts. They waited in turn and Tom heard the woman who stabbed her husband be convicted and sentenced to be hung. They led her off weeping bitterly. Then it was their turn. The jury had found them both guilty of stealing six fowls but had acquitted them of the other charges of damaging property, due to the statement of the local constable, saying he had seen no evidence of this.

"Tom Finnimore and John Martin: You have both been found guilty of each stealing 6 fowls from Farmer Robert Spart. This is a despicable crime that has badly affected this worthy man's livelihood. You are each sentenced to seven years transportation to New South Wales. Prior to this, you will be held in custody in HMS Captivity, off Devonport Docks."

Tom hung his head in despair. Seven years! He might never see his family or England again. He had heard dreadful tales of the ships used to transport convicts to Australia. Often, either the ships or their passengers didn't survive the crossing. What he feared as much, however, was the thought of imprisonment on one of the 'hulks'. Filthy, disease-ridden and brutal – that's all he had ever heard of them. However, he also breathed a very small sigh of relief – he wasn't going to be hung, thank goodness. And maybe a new country would give him a new start. But then he remembered his family, and in spite of himself, the tears rolled silently down his face.

They were taken away from the courtroom to a small jail room where their best Sunday clothes were taken from them to be given to a more deserving person, and they were dressed in prison overalls. This upset Tom more than anything as he remembered what pride his mother had always taken in providing them with decent clothes for Sundays. Now, like everything else, they were gone.

Tom caught sight of his father's horrified face as he left the court. He never had the chance to say goodbye, and he prayed in his heart that his family knew he loved them. This was the end of his old way of life.

Chapter 5

A week later, Tom and John, amongst others, were loaded onto a horse and cart, hands chained, and taken away to HMS Captivity, moored off Devonport. The last week had been a miserable one, spent in a small local gaol house crowded with other prisoners, where they were forced to be silent 24 hours a day. The cells were bare and cold, and the prisoners spent their days scrubbing floors or walking on a treadmill. The food consisted of basic dry biscuits, gruel and water. However, now that was over and they were on their way to the hulks. As they approached Devonport Docks after the eight-hour journey, Tom could see a line of large wooden ships, with no sails, moored along the bank. The horse and cart pulled up alongside one. As Tom gazed upwards at the sides of the ship it was like looking at a monstrous fortress. It rose above him, dark and forbidding. These ships had long ceased to be seaworthy and had a sad and derelict look. Their rigging was hung with grimy items of clothing and bedding. The linen smocks that the convicts were made to wear were of a grey hue from constant dirt and hard use and looked like ghosts on the rigging lines. Then, to his horror, they were ordered to climb up the ladder to go aboard. As he climbed, a dreadful smell hit Tom's nostrils and he nearly retched. It was the smell of human sweat, dirt and hardship, and Tom guessed he would soon smell as bad.

As soon as the new arrivals had got on board they were stripped and washed in two large tubs of cold water. Tom found this humiliating as it took place, publicly, on the top deck of the ship. Then they were dressed in the standard hulk clothing – a coarse linen shirt, a brown jacket and a pair of breeches. They were allowed to keep their own shoes. They were then chained, both hands and feet, and taken below to the cells on either side of the lower decks. These held about 10-16 prisoners each.

Tom soon found the chains were far too tight and were cutting into his arms and legs. When he tried to speak to one of the soldiers guarding them about it, he just laughed sardonically and walked away, saying, "Complain any more, mate, and you'll really find out what pain is!"

Because it was daytime, most of the fellow inmates were over at the shore working. They wouldn't return until nearly 6 o' clock in the evening. The new arrivals were issued hammocks for sleeping in each night and shown where to stow them away in the daytime. The guards instructed them on the daily routine and told them the rules. There was not a trace of humanity in any of their faces. They'd seen too much and been hardened to it. The suffering of the prisoners meant nothing to them; in fact, many of them even revelled in it. As Tom was taken around the beast of a ship he was shocked to see rats running around everywhere, and sick men lying down on the floor, uncared for. As they went onto another deck there were also some human heaps lying covered in a corner, not moving. These poor unfortunates had died where they lay and not been removed. Tom shuddered to think of the diseases there must be around and tried to stay as far away as possible. He thought to himself, that in order to survive, he must keep himself as clean and well fed as possible. It was his only chance. He figured that if he tried to co-operate, work hard and behave well, maybe he would earn a little leniency from the guards. He couldn't expect much, he knew that.

Then all the new arrivals were taken up to the upper deck and told to remove their hats. They then had to parade around, still in irons, so that their faces and appearance could become familiar to the guards. This would happen every day for the first two weeks. Today Tom found it exhausting. The chains weighed him down and he stumbled at times. The weather was cold, misty and damp, and he was soon soaked through his thin shirt. After the parade they were all sent to wash down the decks. Luckily the exercise warmed Tom up and dried his clothes. He worked hard and later in the day, the same soldier who had threatened him earlier, came and loosened his irons which eased Tom's pain considerably.

The rest of the convicts returned at about 6 pm and then Tom really saw what life was going to be like. They were all given boiled ox cheek and potatoes for their evening meal, and then herded up together to 'school' for the evening. Here they learnt to read from the bible and count. Some lessons in writing were also given, but Tom couldn't get the hang of how to hold the quill, so they gave up with him. He'd never been given one before and didn't know what to do with it. This was followed by chapel with prayers. They were then mustered on deck and led down below for the night. Tom had never seen so many people together in such a confined place. They were a rough looking lot.

Occasionally, he saw John in the crowd but mostly they were separated. They were pushed roughly into the cells with about 15 other men, and had to find a space to hang their hammocks. Tom soon found this was far from easy as there was a distinct pecking order already. He nearly got hammered by one of the other inmates for trying to hang his hammock in *his* space. He only escaped a nasty battering by backing down immediately and apologising. Eventually, he found a few feet of space and tried to settle down for the night. However, the cell was far from quiet at first. There was swearing and fights breaking out. Two convicts came to blows as one had stolen another one's shoes. Tom realised he needed to keep a low profile. Sleeping in irons wasn't easy either and certainly not comfortable. Nonetheless, after the guards gave their final shout, silence fell and sleep eventually overcame him. He dreamt he was trying to get to his family, but something kept getting in the way, and the harder he tried, the further away they got. He awoke in the night briefly, remembering where he was and what he had dreamed. This made him feel very sad, but he was determined not to shed any more tears. In here it was a sign of weakness which could be used against him, and Tom didn't want that.

Unbeknown to Tom, things were happening at home on his behalf. On the way home from the trial his father was angry and upset by the verdict and expressed his feelings to the vicar.

"He's just a foolish boy," he said. "He didn't mean to do it. I wish something could be done."

"Well, it can," mused Reverend Ellicombe. "Lots of people appeal against their sentences and sometimes they get reduced or dropped."

Richard Finnimore stared at him, hardly believing his ears. "You mean, things can be changed? Surely, whatever they decide goes?"

"Not necessarily," he replied. "A petition can be sent up to Whitehall to request clemency, and quite often they are successful. Many people, sentenced to transportation, I've heard, never actually go."

Tom's father sighed. "I would never be able to do all that," he said. "I can't even write. I wouldn't know where to start."

The Reverend reassured him, "I can help you write up the details for the petition, then we go to a local lawyer and he'll send it up to Whitehall."

"A lawyer," said Richard doubtfully. "But I don't have any money for that."

"Ah, but the parish has a fund to help the poor," replied the vicar. "And I feel this would be a justified use of some of the money. There's a very good man we have used before for this sort of thing, called William Benidon. I'll contact him. The only thing is, we only have two weeks to get the appeal in."

So it was that Reverend Ellicombe and Richard Finnimore spent the next two evenings compiling all the details of Tom's crime and its mitigating circumstances into a readable account to be taken to the lawyer. They included all the details of Tom's good character that the vicar had been prepared to speak about at the trial, but never got the chance to. The vicar then took it to Mr Benidon, who put it into the necessary legal terms.

It was then sent up to Whitehall and reached it just in the nick of time on the 13th of January 1834. Then the waiting started.

After a week or two, Tom was beginning to settle into the daily routine of the hulks. Each morning, they would be roused at 5.30 am and called up for a basic breakfast of (often mouldy) biscuits and gruel. Then they had to wash down the decks, which Tom didn't mind too much. It gave him time to talk to some of the others, although voices had to be kept low. The guards were quite likely to make them do it all again if they thought they hadn't done it well enough or if they were just in a bad mood. He got to know two or three of the quieter prisoners and also had a chance to say hello to John again, although he didn't get a lot of response. From what Tom could see, John had started to align himself with the rougher convicts and was frequently getting into fights. He nodded to Tom occasionally but showed no inclination to pursue their previous friendship.

After the washing of the decks, the prisoners stowed away their hammocks and then were taken ashore to work. All of them were in irons which made it difficult to walk. Tom's ankles were chafed and sore to start with, although the skin became hard after a time and he ceased to notice the shackles any more. Once ashore, in working parties of ten, they were put to useful labour in the docks, either for the army or for loading and unloading barges in the mud. Tom hated working in the mud, and once was horrified to see a man sink and disappear in it never to be seen alive again. No one could save him. This annoyed the overseer no end as any missing man (be they live or dead) had to be accounted for. If the overseer was angry they all suffered as they got no break at noon and consequently no food. The overseers often liked to treat them that way anyway just to make life even harder.

The work for the army often involved building mounds for artillery practice. This was back breaking work, moving endless mounds of earth and rocks from place to place. Tom's muscles got large and strong, but he ached in places he didn't know he had. The best work of all was working for the various tradesmen around the docks. This could be varied and occasionally interesting. Most of the tradesmen treated them very badly though, even flogging them if they were too slow or clumsy in their work. There was one, however, a Mr Woodford, who gave Tom some respect once he saw how well he worked, and he asked for him sometimes in his working party. On one particularly busy day, he even gave Tom an extra piece of bread, but then the guard saw and warned Mr Woodford not to do that again.

"Don't go giving the scum extra," he growled. "It only makes 'em soft and greedy. They don't deserve nothing!"

After the midday break (if they got it), they worked on until quarter to six. Then they were mustered again and returned to the dreadful ogre of the ship. Tom hated the return as it meant being confined in chains again with hundreds of people like himself – lost, broken, often angry and violent souls, all trying to survive. Survival was certainly hard. Many sickened and died, and nothing was done for them. Disease was rampant as the sick were not kept apart and, as Tom had seen, even corpses were not removed for days. At night, he felt the rats running over him which made him feel repulsed. There was something about them which he abhorred. It may only have been the association with disease, but he found them disgusting. He was terrified they would bite him.

Sunday was at least, partly, a day of rest, without the forced labour. There were Sunday prayers and an inspection of health, clothing and cleanliness. Saturday evening was always the time when they had the chance, just once a week, to wash and shave. Tom always did this as thoroughly as he was allowed. Unfortunately, there were always so many people to get through that time for this was strictly limited.

Occasionally, on Sundays, a few brave visitors came to see people. One Sunday, about two weeks after Tom had arrived there, he was surprised to hear his name called by the guard.

"Finnimore! Come 'ere. It's your lucky day. You got a visitor."

Tom could hardly believe it as he was led into one of the smaller cabins where his older brother Richard was waiting to see him.

"Dick!" he cried. "How wonderful to see you. Is everyone alright at home?"

Dick was quite shocked to see Tom in prison rags, chained by the feet and looking quite haggard in the face. He greeted him warmly. The guard stood outside. They were only allowed half an hour together. Dick reassured Tom about the family and enquired how he was. Tom replied he was getting by. The main reason Dick had come, of course, was to tell Tom that they had sent a petition to Whitehall to try and plead for clemency. Tom was surprised and pleased.

"I didn't know there was such a thing," he said.

"The vicar told us about it," said Dick. "And he and Pa have worked really hard on it. We don't know what will happen, but we wanted you to know there may be some hope."

However, Dick also wanted to tell Tom some news of his own. "I'm moving away," he said, "to London. I've heard there's a new leather market in Bermondsey and lots of work to be had. I'm taking my wife Eliza up with me. I reckon it's a great opportunity."

He was very enthusiastic and Tom wished him well, but his heart sank at the thought of Dick moving away so far. *I will never see him,* he thought. It had taken Dick eight hours to get to Devonport from Exeter by stagecoach, so how long would it take from London? It didn't bear thinking about.

"When you get back," said Dick, "come and find me and I'll get you some work."

They chatted briefly about the family, but all too soon it was over and Dick had to leave. He gave him some home baked bread and a warm coat, but Tom was sure he wouldn't be able to hang on to that for long. He ate most of the bread straight away, savouring the much missed taste and smell of his mother's home cooking. He tucked the last of it inside his shirt for later. He hugged Dick briefly and thanked him for coming, sending love to all the family. The news about the appeal had raised his spirits, though he was frightened to hope too much. Later that night, whilst he lay in his hammock, his new coat was indeed taken from him by the roughest convict of the lot, Ted. Tom protested briefly but after a hefty thump to the stomach, gave in and let it go.

Chapter 6

Towards the end of January Tom, had further good news. One day, one of the guards came in and shouted, "Finnimore! Come 'ere."

People were often being called out and they were then shipped out to New South Wales or removed elsewhere. Tom feared it might be his turn and thought it would be dreadful if his appeal was too late to stop it. However, the guard took him to one of the officers who had something to read to him:

To W Benidon Esq, Exeter   *From Whitehall 27*

Jan 1834

Sir
I am directed by Lord Melbourne to acknowledge receipt of your letter of the 13th Inst with the enclosed petition in favour of Thomas Finnimore, who was convicted at the last quarter session for the County of Devon of stealing fowls, and sentenced to seven years transportation. I am to acquaint you that under all the circumstances of this case his Lordship will feel warranted in giving orders for the removal of the prisoner to the Central Penitentiary at the first convenient opportunity, for confinement for a limited period, instead of being transported.
I am yours,
J H Phillipps

Tom was overjoyed – no more fear of transportation, journeying on a ship for six to eight months to an unknown and harsh new world. The only thing he wanted to know was how long did they mean by 'a limited period'? Was it months, years? The officer said he didn't know. He would just have to wait and see.

Tom's mind raced and he felt in turmoil inside. Surely it wouldn't be long, he reasoned. They had obviously understood that he hadn't meant to do it. But time went by and nothing changed. Tom alternated between hope and despair. It was almost worse to have freedom so close and yet so far.

It was now three months since Tom had started his sentence. The weather was steadily improving, and the cold and damp which had plagued him at first was easing. Towards the end of March, there was another shout of "Finnimore!"

This time, Tom was sure he was going to be released, but no! He was to be taken off to a new hulk called the Leviathan. This was in Portsmouth, so there was no hope whatsoever of any family being able to visit. It was too far. Tom was to leave on the following morning but he was sad to hear that many of the other convicts, John included, were now to be shipped off to New South Wales. He determined to try and speak to John, if only to say goodbye.

The chance came whilst they were washing the decks down that day. Tom saw him and managed to sidle over closer.

"John!" he called under his breath. "It's me, Tom. How are you? I heard you're off soon."

John looked up and Tom saw his face was covered in bruises and scars. He'd been fighting again.

"Yeah," he said. "And I'm glad about it! I need a new chance away from this lot." His face softened and he said quietly. "I tell you what Tom, I wish we never done what we did, but there's no going back. I'm sorry we fell out. Let's part as mates at least."

"I'm sorry too," said Tom. "And I wish you well. I hope you have a safe journey." They shook hands briefly and then parted. Tom never saw John again, but felt better that something had been resolved between them.

The next day, Tom was taken by horse and cart to Portsmouth. He was depressed at the thought of another 'hulk.' The journey was very long and uncomfortable, and all the convicts were chained hand and foot throughout. When they stopped at last, Tom could hardly stand up. His hands and feet were numb. For all intents and purposes the Leviathan was a carbon copy of the HMS Captivity with the same daily routine, the same rats and dysentery rampaging through the ship. The only reason they'd been moved was that the Captivity was used more for short term holding, and the Leviathan was for longer terms. This made Tom feel really low in spirits. Was he going to be here for his full seven years? If only he knew.

Occasionally, Tom passed a few words with the other inmates. One day, he saw a man nearly fainting with overwork and hunger and went to help him. He gave him a bit of his bread which he had left and said a few words of encouragement. The man thanked him and smiled briefly. Only a few moments after Tom turned back to his work, however, another man, of a rougher looking disposition, pulled him over to one side and warned him.

"Don't get tangled up with 'im," said the man. "He's one of them Tolpuddle lot!"

"What's that?" said Tom.

"Ain't you heard? There's been a group of 'em trying to get better wages or something, and they got some sort of workers union going. They've all ended up in here, so that just shows you, don't it? Doesn't pay to cross the masters. You watch out. If the guards think you're in with them, you'll suffer!"

Tom made a mental note not to talk to the Tolpuddle man again. He couldn't risk anything. He felt sorry for him though and a bit guilty.

Three more months of hell went by. Tom had a fever for a week but luckily it wasn't dysentery, only a chill brought on by poor food and lack of proper clothing. The officers on this hulk often pocketed the money allocated for the prisoners' clothing, so they went without. Tom had no jacket, a ripped shirt and shoes that had holes in them, but this was typical. The officers on the Leviathan were even more corrupt than those on the Captivity, if that was possible. The convicts were on the most basic diet possible, with meat served only once a week. Rice with treacle was often their evening meal, which filled their bellies but was not nourishing. Convicts were dying in their dozens.

Tom lay in his hammock, alternately shivering and burning. Every limb ached and his eyes and nose streamed. The guards came by and swore and shouted at him to try to get him out to work. Tom groaned loudly and clutched his stomach, so they thought he had the dreaded dysentery with its violent diarrhoea and sickness. Fortunately, therefore, they left him well alone. Tom felt justified in a bit of exaggeration as he knew that if he didn't rest he would get worse and could die. He was determined to get well and made sure he staggered out each evening for some food and water. After a few days he pulled himself together and got up.

One day, at the end of July 1834, Tom was once again shouted for. His hopes went up. Surely this was it, he would be released. Unfortunately, these hopes were soon dashed yet again. He was just being moved to Millbank Penitentiary in London to serve out the rest of his sentence, however long the authorities deemed that to be. At least he would be away from the hulks, he thought. Surely things must improve?

Chapter 7

Millbank was certainly different to the hulks, but as to whether it was an improvement, Tom wasn't so sure. He was led through its long dark corridors and twisting passages to a single bare cell. Compared with the crowded and noisy hulks where he was crammed in with 15 other convicts, this seemed like luxury to start with. It was clean and there were no rats running around, so he was grateful for that. His cell contained a washing tub, a stool, hammock and bedding and a couple of prayer books. There was a window, but it was only a tiny slit, very high up looking out into a grey, stone courtyard. There were two doors, both firmly bolted behind him.

The main problem was the silence. Tom discovered that this prison was run on the 'silence and separation' policy. This meant that the prisoners were forced to be totally silent 24 hours a day. The theory was that the convicts would be able to reflect on their sins and repent. Even so, this didn't totally work as several prisoners had gone mad recently and two had killed themselves. Tom didn't know any of this, but on the first day, he heard distant screams from around the prison which sounded inhuman and desperate. As he was locked in his cell for the first time, he felt the silence closing in around him like a thick cloak. It was almost palpable. He read the prison rules, which were on the wall, and was pleased to see that good conduct and hard work could lead to extra benefits or even a remission in sentence. He was determined to work hard and do well. However, he also read that any infringement of the silence rule would be dealt with severely, by whippings, chains or reduced food rations. But at night, the whispering started. The lights went out and all over the prison Tom could hear people talking softly. The prison was so badly designed that noise carried all over it and despite the guards shouting at people, it was impossible to stop all communication. In the daytime, the guards could identify and punish the guilty parties, but at night it was unfeasible. Tom settled down in his hammock, but just as he did he heard a whistle and a low voice from the cell next door.

"Hello. Who are you? Are you new here?"

Tom got out and went over to the wall where the voice was loudest.

"Hello," he whispered, being careful to keep his voice as low as possible. "I'm Tom, just arrived. Shouldn't we be silent? Won't the guards hear us?"

"They can't do nothing at night," replied the mysterious voice. "'cept shout at us, that is! They can't tell who's who. My name's Joe Harvey and I'm in for burglary. What about you?"

"The same," replied Tom. "But it was only six chickens."

"Don't matter what it is," said Joe. "The judges love to punish people. It's their job! Where you come from?"

So Tom ended up telling Joe about himself and his home in Alphington. Joe in return told Tom about his previous life in Norfolk. Joe was philosophical about his punishment.

"I deserved it," he said. "Was my own fault. I got left in charge of a shop and I got tempted by the till. I didn't hurt nobody, at least!"

This was a friendship that was to sustain Tom throughout his time in Millbank, even though he never knew what Joe looked like. They talked most nights and it became something they both looked forward to – some human communication. Tom reflected that you didn't need to see someone's face in order to be friends with them. It was a friendship born out of necessity, but also out of mutual interests. They both came from farming backgrounds and hoped to improve their lot when they got out. Joe wanted to be a shopkeeper (as he reckoned he knew how to look after his own till), and Tom was seriously considering his brother's offer in the leather market. But the future still seemed a very long way off at present.

Joe had a ready laugh and an easygoing manner. He shrugged off the imprisonment like it was just another phase of life. Tom took it harder and longed for freedom, but Joe helped him accept it as much as possible.

During the days, the convicts were allocated work such as tailoring, weaving, shoe making, rug making etc. This was usually done in their own cells, although a few trades required them to work in association with others. As Tom had had a small amount of experience with leather they gave him shoe making to do. He had to sit for hours in his dimly lit cell, bent over pieces of leather, sewing them together. In spite of this, whilst he worked his mind was free to wander wherever it liked, and mostly it went back to his home in Alphington. He remembered the fertile fields and the rolling Devon hills he had always loved. He also remembered playing down by the Alphin Brook when he was little. In his memories, the sun always seemed to be shining and the family was happy and healthy. He knew it probably bore little resemblance to reality, but it was a pleasant way to while away the time. Occasionally his thoughts also strayed towards Mary Ann, and who could really blame him? He had never felt that way about anyone before. He still missed them all desperately, although he was, against all the odds, surviving.

Once a day, the convicts were exercised by walking silently around the yard or on the treadmill. They also had to go to 'school' and chapel. Chapel was the only time they were allowed to use their voices in order to praise God in song. They sang lustily, just in order to hear themselves again. Disease also occasionally did the rounds of Millbank, in particular, scurvy and dysentery due to the poor diet. The food seemed mostly to consist of bread, with a small amount of boiled beef and potatoes. The meat had been boiled so long it tasted of nothing anymore and it made Tom long for home cooking. Joe had been there longer than Tom and had now earned himself a few privileges for good behaviour. He was allowed out into the courtyard to work as a mason and saw more of what was going on in the prison. In the evenings, he regaled Tom with amusing tales of the prison guards or other prisoners. Tom wished he could see something other than the same cell all the time. He was heartily sick of it, and found the exercise time very welcome. He also wished he knew what Joe looked like and tried to picture him in his mind. He knew he must be among the men attending chapel, but as the prisoners were not all let out of the cells at the same time, he could only guess which face might be his.

Time went by and Tom also managed to earn himself a few privileges. He was given a badge of good conduct which he wore proudly. His diet improved slightly, he was allowed an extra book and he was allocated to work a few hours a week in the prison allotment. Tom loved this. He had always enjoyed growing things and this got him out into the open air; not that the air around Millbank could be described as 'fresh' as the prison was situated on marsh land and was therefore damp and unhealthy. Nevertheless, Tom prospered and the guards were impressed with him.

One day, in one of his conversations with Joe, he heard that Joe was going to be released next week. He had served his time. Tom was pleased for him, but devastated at the thought of losing his only friend. He didn't know how he would cope and he said so to Joe.

"Cheer up, mate!" said Joe. "It'll be your turn next. Won't be long now."

Tom hoped he was right. He listened to Joe excitedly making plans for the future and wished him lots of luck. If only his turn would come as well, he thought. Joe left in February 1837 and Tom was bereft. No one else moved in next door, and after a month of utter loneliness he was getting desperate. His mind just went over and over things when he was in his hammock at night and he could hardly sleep. Luckily, his time out on the allotment helped save his sanity.

Then came the much longed for day at the beginning of April that year, just as Tom was beginning to wonder how much more he could take. A guard called for him and took him to the governor. Tom had only met the governor once before and this was on the day he arrived. He appeared to be a cold, hard-hearted man, but this time he was smiling as he read to Tom that at last he was to be granted a free pardon and was going to be released. Finally, the time had come and Tom could start a new life as a free man.

Chapter 8
London, 1837

It was a beautiful spring morning when the huge front gate of the prison opened and Tom stepped out into the outside world. He looked around but there was no one waiting for him. He hadn't really expected anyone, but was disappointed all the same. He walked a few yards along the road, but then had to sit down on a low wall, feeling completely overwhelmed. After the perpetually silent twilight world of the prison, the bright light and the noise of the London streets seemed too much. It bombarded his senses from all sides and he couldn't take it. He felt dizzy and faint, and had to put his head in his hands to ease the pain. Even the prison allotment had been surrounded by high, forbidding, grey walls, so very little light penetrated there. His eyes stung and watered, and his ears rang. There were people shouting, dogs barking, horses and carts clattering by and workers going about their business. All seemed totally unaware of Tom. He sat there for what seemed like ages, until bit by bit, he was able to uncover his head and get accustomed to the light and the noise. He tried to stand up after a while, but still felt faint so sat down again and had something to eat.

Yesterday, the prison chaplain, the Reverend Daniel Nihil, had come to Tom's cell, congratulated him on his pardon and then proceeded to lecture him at length on the value of leading a virtuous life. Firstly, he gave him a copy of the letter which proclaimed his pardon in case he ever needed to prove it. Then he led Tom in prayers for the redemption of his soul and forgiveness of his previous sins. Tom went along with it all as he knew it was useless to argue. The chaplain had a lot of authority in the prison and it was strongly rumoured that he might even be the next governor. No one disagreed with him if they knew what was good for them.

After the lengthy sermon and prayers the chaplain finally gave Tom something else of use. The charitable ladies of the Prisoner's Aid Society provided each discharged prisoner with some basic civilian clothing, some food and a small amount of money, which Tom received now. The money was supposed to get the ex-convicts back home again, but looking at it, Tom knew it wasn't enough to be able to buy a stagecoach ticket to Devon. He'd been thinking about what to do and thought maybe he would try and find his brother, Dick. He didn't have an address, but he knew he was working at Bermondsey Leather Market so he reckoned he should be able to find him there. The only trouble was Tom didn't know London at all, and had no idea where Bermondsey was in relation to Millbank or how far. So he asked Reverend Nihil for help with this and the chaplain did his best to explain where it was to Tom.

"It's about three miles away," he said. "You'll need to cross the river. Probably Westminster Bridge is best, or you could use the Horseferry at Lambeth, but that costs a bit."

To give him his due, the chaplain got a piece of paper and drew a rough map for Tom. Although Tom couldn't read very well, he was able to understand the diagram and he started to look at it now. The chaplain had advised him to follow the riverbank until he reached the bridge and then cross over.

Tom felt better and started to walk slowly in the sunshine, trying to take everything in. Growing up in rural Devon, he had never imagined anywhere so big and bustling. He came across huge, grand buildings, and also poverty-stricken slums. There seemed such a contrast between the rich and the poor here, more so than at home. He wondered how the poor survived. Walking on, he saw the grand Westminster Abbey, which he had heard about but never imagined he would see. It rose above him, tall and magnificent, but, he reflected, it was not for the likes of him. On the other side of the road were the burnt out ruins of the Houses of Parliament, the Palace of Westminster. A fire had broken out one day in October 1834, just after Tom had entered Millbank, and all this time later, people were still arguing about how to rebuild it. Tom wondered where his petition had gone to; was it there? If so, it was just in time. Mentally, he thanked the person who had had enough insight to accept the appeal.

Tom crossed Westminster Bridge, looking at the great River Thames, which was crowded with vessels of all kinds. It was impressive in its size and majesty, but the water looked brown and dirty, not like the fresh running Devon rivers he had been used to. There were also lumps of what appeared to be human sewage floating in it. Not only that, but the very air was thick with smoke and soot from newly developed industries, and Tom soon found it was in his hair and on his skin. The sun struggled to break through the smog in places.

By now Tom was feeling tired and hungry. Walking along London streets made him feel exhausted. The sights, sounds and smells of such a mass of humanity took a lot of getting used to. Just about then he came upon one of London's small green areas and gratefully turned into a courtyard to rest and recuperate. There was only some rough, patchy grass and a couple of stunted trees, but to Tom it seemed like paradise. He took off his shoes and let his feet feel real grass for the first time in ages. A feeling of pure happiness came over him. Not a soul in the world knew where he was. He was free at last and could relax. No one could take this moment away from him.

After a time, Tom moved on and continued his walk through Southwark and on to Bermondsey. He was shocked by the squalid, dirty slums that he saw. He had always thought that London was prosperous. The river front was slimy and treacherous with precarious wooden shacks built out over it, housing the poorest of the poor. Tom remembered the convict sinking in the mud when he was in the hulks and he shuddered.

Further inland he finally came to the grand front entrance of the new leather market on Weston Street. He could smell it before he could see it. The stench of blood and skins permeated the whole area. As he went down the road towards it he passed enormous buildings which could only be tanneries. Tom was amazed at the amount of them there were. Obviously the trade was flourishing. He went through the entrance into the large space inside, but then stopped as if there was a physical barrier.

There were hundreds of people working there. The bustle and the noise were tremendous. Tom felt a rising wave of panic come upon him, and he could hardly breathe. He flattened himself against a wall, his breath coming in gasps, feeling quite faint. He simply wasn't used to crowds any more, after three years of mostly solitary confinement. However, Tom was no quitter. He knew he had to find his brother and hoped he was here somewhere. He edged along the outside of the yard, clutching at walls in order to give himself something solid to hang on to. There were so many people – how was he ever going to find the one person he wanted to see? Everyone looked alike. They all had overalls and working clothes on and many wore hats as well, so it was difficult to see their faces. Tom decided he would have to pluck up courage and ask around. The first man he approached just shrugged and walked off, which wasn't encouraging. All the same, if he was to have anywhere to sleep tonight, he needed to find his brother, so he kept trying. Tom fought his panic and fear down, and moved around.

Eventually, one man replied – "Oh, you want Dicky Finnimore? He's over by the vats on the right, mate. Can't miss him."

Tom made his way over and suddenly saw him. "Dick," he cried. "It's me, Tom. I'm free!"

Dick was delighted to see him, enfolding him in a great bear hug. He insisted Tom come back to the house with him to meet his wife Eliza, get some food and rest. Tom was heartily glad to leave the crowded market behind and get some peace and quiet. Dick took him to a small terraced house just behind the market. On the way, he bombarded Tom with questions – when did he get out? How was he? What were his plans? But Tom couldn't answer at that moment. He needed time to clear his head and rest. After a few minutes, Dick realised this and was quiet. He left him with Eliza, a plump, pleasant, homely sort of woman with a ready smile and a welcoming manner. She sat Tom down, got him food and drink then left him to rest.

The next thing Tom knew he was waking up after a long nap, just as Dick was getting home for the day. He felt better now and ready to talk. He and Dick talked well into the evening about Tom's experiences, his plans, plus the family at home. Tom was anxious to know how they all were.

Dick told him that Will and John had now moved out.

"Will's up here in London as well," he said. "We'll get him over and you can see him. John's got a fishmongers shop in Alphington, both of them married now of course, and Will's got a couple of kids already. Pa's not well though and can't work much. Lizzie does her best to help out and Ma's taking in washing to make ends meet. I send them some money when I can and so does Will, but times are hard for them."

"I want to go home and see them," said Tom. "But I don't have much money. I don't know how much the stage costs."

"I can give you the money," said Dick. "But if you are thinking of trying to stay and earn a living down there, I warn you, there's not a lot of work there at the moment. There's a lot of new farm machinery coming in which is taking people's jobs. Some farmers have gone under recently, and wages have gone down instead of up."

"I'm not sure what to do," said Tom. "Maybe I could join you up here if you think I could get a job. The only thing is, I can't cope with all those crowds in the market!"

He felt really embarrassed to talk about it, but he had to explain about his feelings of panic that afternoon. Dick understood though and reassured him, saying it was only natural after years inside prison.

"Look," he said. "I know a small tannery on the edge of the market which needs more men. I'll have a word with the manager, I know him well; he's a friend of mine. You could start at the bottom and work your way up. It's good regular work, and being a small business, it won't be so busy."

Tom agreed it was probably worth a try, but was keen to visit home first and see the family. Privately, Tom thought to himself that it was ironic that he was thinking of going into tanning, as it was that that had caused his problems in the first place. Nowadays, however, he was no longer so fussy about what he did. Prison had certainly cured him of that. He would be happy just to be working and earning a living again.

Dick said he would book him a ticket for the stagecoach in a few days' time, then Tom could have a rest before undertaking such a long, arduous journey. He insisted Tom stay with them, so Eliza made him up a bed in the spare room. That night, Tom found it really hard to sleep. It had been three and a half years since he last slept in an actual bed and it felt strange. The blankets were too warm and the mattress too soft. He almost missed the feel of a hammock. When he rose the next morning, out of habit he stripped the bedding off, neatly folded it and stowed it away in a corner. Eliza laughed when she saw it.

"You don't have to do that no more, Tom! You're with family now."

Tom laughed and relaxed. It was good to feel wanted. The old prison habits died hard, however, and at breakfast Tom ate fast, licking his plate clean of every last bit, not realising that there was no longer any need.

"Slow down!" said Eliza. "There's no rush. Plenty more if you want it."

Tom reddened. "I'm sorry," he said. "It's gonna take a bit of getting used to."

"It's okay," she replied kindly. "Take your time, no problem."

The next few days were a valuable time of adjustment for Tom. He learnt to sleep in a real bed, eat meals at a normal pace and talk to people again. Will and his family came around one evening, and they all reminisced about the past and made plans for the future. Tom felt truly happy again.

Chapter 9

A couple of days after that, Tom left London on the stagecoach for Devon. The railways were developing faster now, but Tom wasn't sure about travelling on such a frightening looking machine, and anyway, routes to Devon were few and far between at present. Stagecoaches were slow but cheap, and they travelled right into Exeter. Dick saw Tom off, giving him enough money for a return fare as well. Tom was still undecided about coming back to London; his heart still belonged to Devon. Dick had spoken to his friend at the tannery and secured a place for Tom if he wanted it; however, he was keeping his options open.

The journey took two days to Exeter as it made frequent stops at coaching inns along the way for the horses and passengers to be refreshed. Tom was impatient to get there and watched out at every stop to see where he was and how close to home. Every mile seemed to take forever. He was stiff and tired when at last he got out at Alphington. Dick had told Tom that the family now lived at 51 Main Street and that it was very basic, so not to expect too much. It was evening when he finally arrived, and there had been no way to let them know to expect him. Tom reached the front door and suddenly felt quite nervous. What would they say to him? How would he fit in? He hesitated a moment, but then their voices reached his ears and the smell of home cooking wafted out, and he could resist no longer. He needn't have worried. As soon as they saw him they fell on him with hugs and kisses. His mother cried with happiness and wouldn't let him move from her side all night. His younger brother and sisters chattered away happily, trying to tell him all their news.

Even his father said gruffly, "It's good to have you home, son."

That first evening back felt enjoyable but strange, tasting his mother's cooking again, talking and telling as much as he could remember about what had happened to him. They could hardly believe him. They, in turn, told him about the village and the people who had come and gone. Mary Ann's family, it seemed, had moved up to Bristol and they'd heard Mary Ann was walking out with a young man up there. Tom felt disappointed, although he hadn't expected anything really, but he had still cherished secret dreams of them being together one day. His sisters Lizzie and Sarah had grown up a lot and had started working. Lizzie also had a young man courting her. They told him tales of people around the village, but he couldn't remember half of them now. His mother looked thin, tired and much older. They had obviously had some hard times. His father moved around painfully and was often out of breath. It made Tom sad to see it. His younger brother, Eddie, had taken on more of the role of the man of the house, doing much of the manual work, even though he was only fifteen. This made Tom feel a bit redundant. Although he was happy to see them all again, he felt out of place and disconnected from the village. Maybe it *was* time to move on?

The next day, Lizzie took Tom around the village and he was surprised to see a lot of changes. It seemed that what his brother Dick had said was true. Alphington's farming community was struggling to survive. Industrialisation was creeping in and people were being replaced by machines. They paid a visit to his brother John's shop and Tom was pleased to see it was busy with customers. At least he was doing well. There seemed to be more shops and businesses than there used to be, but the traditional rural way of life was declining. Tom wondered what kind of occupation he could do if he stayed around here. He enquired if John needed any help; he said he was sorry but he couldn't afford to pay anyone else. Tom also enquired in several other places, but the answer was the same – no money. He also asked at the rope makers if there was any work and they said there might be a chance. When they asked Tom what he had been doing, however, he was forced to admit he'd been in prison, and they promptly told him to go away. He was not the kind of person they wanted to employ. Alphington still had very traditional values. Tom wondered if London would be more tolerant of people's mistakes.

Whilst they were out, they also paid a visit to Reverend Ellicombe as his father had told Tom that he had helped with the petition. Although the vicar was pleased to see Tom, he was very busy with a forthcoming wedding service and so was unable to talk. Tom was able to thank him briefly, but was left feeling unsatisfied as he would have liked to have said more. He wasn't sure if the right words would have come anyway, as he was finding it difficult to communicate properly at the moment.

He just blurted out, "Sir! It's me, Tom Finnimore. You helped me. I wanted to thank you."

"That's alright, my son," the vicar replied. "Good luck with everything." Then he turned away.

It was soon obvious that Tom couldn't stay at home. For one thing, there was very little room in the cottage, and for another, there wasn't enough money to feed another mouth. There was also now a strange distance between him and the rest of them. Too much had happened to him that they couldn't understand. They seemed to think he could just be the same old Tom like before, but he was changed by his experiences. He was quieter and more serious, haunted by bad dreams of the past three years. Sometimes he woke up in a cold sweat in the night, thinking he was still on the hulks with the rats running over him. He, in turn, couldn't understand village life any more. The local gossip did not interest him. It seemed so trite and meaningless. Having seen life at its bleakest, he could not connect with such triviality. He would have found it all amusing before, but his struggle for existence had taken its toll. It was ironic really, because all the time in prison he had been thinking of them and longing to go home, but now he was here, he knew he didn't belong any more.

One evening, his father asked him what his plans were for the future, and it was clear from his tone of voice that he felt it was time for Tom to be moving on. Tom felt now was the time to have a heart to heart with his father.

"Pa," he said. "I am really grateful to you for appealing against my sentence for me. I know it took a lot of effort and it really paid off. Now I feel I need to earn a living and the best place to do that is in London with Dick. He's said he can find me a place there in the tanning business."

"Yes, I think that's best," agreed his father. "But I know your mother will be disappointed. She wants you to settle down here; but to be honest, lad, there's nothing much 'round here at the moment. You know we'd love to have you stay, but we just can't. I'm sorry."

Tom told his mother that evening that he was moving up to London permanently.

His mother started crying and said, "Oh, Tom, we've only just got you back and now you're going again. Please stay. We need you!"

Her tears moved him and he put his arms around her. "I love you, Ma, but I need to go. I can't help you by being here. There's just not enough work. If I work with Dick I can send you some money to help out. At the moment, I'm just a drain on you."

His mother protested tearfully but knew it was the truth. Tom had to make his own way in the world now. Next day, he booked his return ticket to London.

Chapter 10

Dick was delighted when Tom arrived back and said he was going to stay. He insisted that Tom live with them as long as he liked.

"We've a spare room and the bit of extra money would help. Then when you get yourself sorted, you're welcome to leave, no problem. I'll let Mr Phillips know you want to start as soon as possible."

Tom's face fell. "The only thing I'm worried about," he said, "is what happens if he finds out about my prison record. He'll want to get rid of me."

Dick laughed. "No one cares about that here in London, Tom. Half the market workers have been inside! No one's bothered. It's a new start for you here. Make the most of it."

Tom was relieved and happily started work a couple of days later. On the first morning, Dick took Tom over to meet his new boss, James Phillips.

"Good morning, sir," said Tom.

"Call me Jim," laughed the man. "We don't stand for no titles 'round 'ere."

Jim was a large, jovial man of around forty years old, with a red face and a rather large belly due to enjoying a few more ales than he should at times.

"What do you know about tanning?" he asked.

"Well," said Tom, "I've spent a short time working in a tannery in Devon, and recently I was making shoes when I was in…er…" he trailed off, not sure of what to say.

"In the clink, you mean!" said Jim, laughing. "Your brother told me all about it. It don't worry me none. Just work hard and keep your nose clean and we'll get on fine. Tell you what – I like my workers to know all the different parts of the business so I'm gonna put you on each area in turn so you can learn all there is to know. Then when you've done that you can move to the thing you're best at. How's that sound?"

"That sounds great," replied Tom. "I'm really keen to learn everything and I promise you, I'll work hard. You won't regret giving me a chance."

"Heh, stop that talk!" said Jim. "You'll make me blush like a girl. Come on, let's get started."

Tom meant what he said. In spite of his original aversion to the tanning industry, he was keen to get on. When he had started work previously, he had found the stench disgusting and the whole process sickening, but having been on the hulks he had now smelt and seen far worse – human waste, human sickness, rotting corpses. At least this process had a positive reason for it – to make leather items for the home and business. Although Tom did not look forward to the stage of soaking the hides in a solution of watered down animal faeces, he figured he could handle it now.

He started his training on the first stage of trimming and splitting the raw hides. The rest of the workforce were a lively bunch and the banter was enjoyable, if a little ripe at times. Tom soon learnt to join in with the rest. He'd only been working there a few weeks when one of the men came in one day, saying, "Hey! What do you think? The old King's kicked the bucket!"

"Great!" exclaimed Jim. "That's good news. It means a public holiday for us all on Coronation day. Who's going to be the new one? Have you heard?"

"They reckon it'll be that girl, Victoria."

"But she's only 18! Well I never."

Jim was right. It was a holiday for most people that day, although it didn't happen for over a year. The months of preparation before the Coronation were frantic in the capital, and all sorts of souvenirs were already on sale. Businesses were determined to make the most of it. By the time the big event arrived, Tom had now moved on to the third stage of the tanning process, that of scraping and scouring the previously soaked hides. He didn't mind that too much. There was a certain amount of satisfaction in seeing the raw skin gradually start to become something like leather. It was the soaking stages he disliked the most, but he had learnt to accept them as a necessary evil.

Thousands of people were coming to London for the Coronation from all over the country, and Tom was overjoyed that some of his family were coming up from Devon. The expansion of the railways meant that travel was now easier and faster. Sarah, Lizzie and Eddie were all coming, but not John as he couldn't get away from the shop. Tom and his brothers were really looking forward to seeing them again. Unfortunately, their parents couldn't make it as their father wasn't well enough to travel and their mother was staying to look after him. Even so, it promised to be a happy reunion. Will and Dick went to collect them from the station. Tom wasn't sure he would be able to cope with all that noise, steam and people. He was a lot better in crowds nowadays and even managed to cross the marketplace when required, but he didn't feel comfortable. It never occurred to him that there would be a lot of people around on Coronation Day, as he was so looking forward to being with his family that, in his mind, they were the only people he would see.

A very, merry evening was had by all when the others arrived. They were staying with Will and his wife, as they had quite a big house now. Will was doing fairly well as a leather dresser these days. He had his own business, which was thriving. Tom was very happy that night having so many of his family together in one place.

The day of the Coronation dawned bright and sunny. The procession was due to go around from Buckingham Palace to Hyde Park Corner, Piccadilly, St James St, Pall Mall, Charing Cross Road and on to Whitehall. This was to give as many members of the public as possible a chance to see it. Tom and his family decided to head for Piccadilly as it seemed to offer a good stretch in which to see the much-rumoured splendour of the gold coach and eight white horses that Victoria would be riding in. They arrived very early in order to try and get a place, but it wasn't long before it was clear that everyone else had the same idea. People were jostling for space and cramming in. Tom began to feel a bit worried at this point, but managed to hold it together.

Dick had forgotten about Tom's problem as it hadn't been mentioned in ages. He led the group of them further forward, trying to get a good spot. Everyone was very excited and had hardly had any breakfast in their rush to get there. They waited a long time, all dressed in their Sunday best, admiring all the rich people in their fine clothes seated on the galleries. The houses, shops and balconies were decorated with bright flags and hangings especially for the occasion, and the whole scene was quite splendid. At about 9 o'clock, however, there was a sudden rush of people from a side street into their part of Piccadilly, and suddenly they were all crushed in even more. The amount of people was tremendous with scarcely room to move. People were in serious danger of being trampled underfoot. Tom, until now, had been sweating profusely and breathing heavily, but he had been trying desperately to focus on his family and the gaiety of the day. Nonetheless, this surge forwards was too much for him, and he knew he couldn't stand any more. He could hardly breathe and he knew he had to get away. Lizzie was standing next to him and was shocked to see Tom suddenly turn in the opposite direction to everyone else. She heard him mutter, "I've got to get out of here!" and then he forced his way through the crowd, desperately.

It felt strange swimming against this tide of humanity. Everyone else was pushing their way forward but he was doing the opposite. People stared at him as if he was mad. Tom didn't care. He was in a cold sweat and couldn't think straight any more. He just knew he had to get out. The crowd very reluctantly parted to let him through.

Some even called abuse at him. "What do you think you're doing, you idiot? Get out the way!"

Finally, Tom reached the back of the crowd and suddenly saw a patch of green ahead of him. It was the corner of Hyde Park. He headed into it thankfully and collapsed on his knees, onto the ground. He sat there, gradually letting his breath return to normal, his head in his hands. Some short time afterwards, he heard a soft voice talking to him. It was Lizzie, his sister, who had followed him as she was worried about him. It had taken a lot of courage to do this, as Lizzie had no knowledge of London, but her fondness for her brother had made her put aside all thoughts of her own safety.

"Tom," she said. "Are you okay? What's wrong?"

Tom was so ashamed and embarrassed.

"Oh Lizzie," he said. "I can't cope with all these people. I thought I could do it but I can't. I'm sorry!"

He hung his head, his face burning with shame. Lizzie said nothing, but just sat and held him like a child in her arms, murmuring gentle soothing sounds.

"It was my time inside," he said when at last he could speak. "The silence, the loneliness – it's ruined me!"

"Hey," said Lizzie. "Enough of that. Let's take it easy. Relax!"

"I'm sorry. I've ruined your day!" said Tom. "You should be there enjoying yourself."

"Come on," said Lizzie. "I'm fine. Let's have a walk around and see if we can see it all from here."

Part of Hyde Park was set up as a fair with stalls, tents, amusements etc. for later in the day, but at this stage, everyone was on the streets and therefore it was quiet. Lizzie led Tom away and up a small hill into the park. After a while, they stopped and turned, looking back, and just at that moment Victoria's coach came by below. They could see everything clearly despite being a distance away, as they were on slightly higher ground. The procession was truly magnificent with the sunlight glinting off the gold of the coach and the horses' bridles. They even caught a brief glimpse of the golden gown of the young queen as the procession flashed past. It was a moment to cherish and remember. The two of them cheered and waved, even though they were the only ones there.

"See," said Lizzie, "we've seen everything after all. You haven't ruined anything."

Tom hugged her. He felt better now and was determined to enjoy the rest of the day. He and Lizzie headed for the fair and were later able to meet up with the others again. Tom was expecting a barrage of questions about his disappearance, but Dick had explained everything, and they were all just pleased to see he was okay. The family had a great time together, trying out all the games and attractions. Once, Tom thought he saw Mary Ann in the distance and his heart leapt. But whoever it was disappeared into the crowd before he could investigate further. He didn't dwell on it for long. That part of his life was gone, he reckoned.

In spite of everything, it had, after all, turned out to be a wonderful day, he thought.

Chapter 11
1842

Time went by and Tom slowly learnt all the stages of the tanning industry. Jim was a good boss to work for; fair with his men, good tempered and jolly. Tom, in return, was a loyal, hardworking employee. For some time, he struggled to get to grips with adding the right amount of oak tannin to the hides and managed to ruin a couple whilst learning. Too much tannin and the hides would harden too much, too little and they could disintegrate. Even so, Jim didn't reprimand or punish him. He simply told Tom that it comes with experience and gave him more chances until he got it right. Eventually, having completed all his training, Tom was given a pay rise and offered the choice of which stage he preferred to do. In fact it was the later stage of softening the hides by beating them with a hammer and then working in oil or tallow by hand that he found the most satisfying. The steady working and rubbing of the leather, watching it slowly come to life as a workable product, was something he enjoyed. He was very happy when Jim agreed that he could work on that stage most of the time as long as he could cover the others if necessary. Tom now decided to move out into his own place. Dick and Eliza were starting a family and would need more of their own space soon, and Tom also felt it was time he was more independent. He settled into a small flat a few houses down the road and started enjoying life as a single man. He was now in his mid-twenties, but there was still no woman in his life. There had been, it was true, the occasional woman of easy morals who had passed through, but there was no one who had captured his heart. Maybe it wouldn't happen, he thought; not everyone marries.

A few months later, in 1842, came the sad news that his father had died. Tom was sad, but not really surprised as he had been ill for a long time. Recently, his parents had been living just with Lizzie looking after them. The others were now all working and settled. Eddie was an agricultural labourer and Sarah was in domestic service. Dick came to see Tom to let him know and they discussed going down for the funeral. Tom decided he really wanted to go to support his mother and to show his respect for his father. Without him, he knew he would have ended up in New South Wales and could have been there still. Dick said he would have to stay in London as Eliza was near her time with their first child, and as she had already had a miscarriage last year, he felt he couldn't leave her. Will was busy at work but would be able to go for a few days. The next day, Tom asked his boss, Jim, and he agreed he could take whatever time he needed, although he would not be paid, of course, whilst he was away. So Tom and Will agreed to travel down together by train.

Travelling by train was all new to Tom and he was rather nervous at first, especially whilst stepping between the platform and the train. There seemed such a big gap he was worried he might fall down it. But once he and Will were settled in their carriage he enjoyed it in spite of himself and was amazed at how quickly the miles sped away.

When they arrived at the cottage they found their mother calm but weary. She had spent so long looking after their father that she was worn out, and it was almost a relief for her now that he was gone. Lizzie was more emotional but held it together for their mother's sake. Tom and Will did their best to help out and comfort them. It was strange being in the family home without their father. There seemed to be a large hole which couldn't be filled. His father had been a rock of stability in times of family crisis, and Tom realised just how much he would miss him. He hadn't seen him much lately, but at least he had always known he was there.

The next day, Tom and Will went over to see the vicar to sort out the last arrangements for the funeral. The Reverend Ellicombe gave them a warm welcome and brought them into the vicarage to discuss the details. It was then that Tom finally got to say what he'd been trying to before, when he first came out of prison.

"Sir," he said, "I really am very grateful to you for all your help in my time of trouble. If it wasn't for you and Pa, who knows what would have happened to me."

"You're very welcome," replied the vicar. "Your father really believed in you and in the fact that it was just a youthful misdemeanour. Your conversation with me beforehand also convinced me of your innate goodness and I was glad to help. Your father was a good man and it's a great loss."

"It is indeed," agreed Tom, and he wished inside that he'd known his father just a bit better.

After their visit to the vicar, Tom and Will headed to the shops to get some provisions. They were walking along to the bakers when they heard a voice call out suddenly – "Tom!"

They turned, and to Tom's surprise they saw Mary Ann coming towards them. She was, if anything, lovelier than ever. She was now a woman in her twenties with a fully developed figure and beauty. Her hair was of a golden blonde and was teased into tiny curls around her face, which was very becoming. Tom was immediately fascinated by her all over again.

He blushed and stammered, "Mary Ann! Hello. How are you?"

"I'm fine," she said, "or I would be if I could get out of this place! I was in Bristol, working at a grand house as a parlour maid. It was so fashionable there. My Master and Mistress held balls and parties all the time, it was wonderful. My Mistress was going to make me her personal ladies maid, but then Mother died and Father decided to come back down here. I have to keep house for him so I had to come too. I really don't think it's very fair. My sister Hannah is still there, but then she's married."

"What about you?" asked Tom, "I heard there was a young man you were seeing?"

"Yes, I was seeing Robert," she said absentmindedly. "But he was boring really. So slow! Anyway, he's still up in Bristol, so that's all over. What are you doing?"

"Well," replied Tom, "I'm working as a tanner up in London. It's good steady work and I'm fully trained now."

"London!" exclaimed Mary Ann. "Oh, I'd love to be up there. It must be so exciting. I really want to move there, but Father won't let me."

"It's not that exciting," said Tom, privately remembering the slums, the dirt and the smell of human decay.

"Oh, you're just used to it!" she said. "I wish I was there."

"Well," said Tom, "you could always come and visit. I could show you the sights. Maybe your father would let you have a holiday."

"Yes," said Will, who had been quiet until now. "I believe you know my wife – Ann Lock, as she used to be – she used to live next door to you. You could always stay with us. We've got three children, but there's still some room to spare. You'd be welcome."

"Oh that'd be wonderful!" cried Mary Ann. "But I'll have to speak to Father. Give me your address so I can write to you and let you know."

"I'm not much of one for reading," said Will, "but Ann's good at it, so I'll give it to her."

They exchanged addresses and then, after expressing brief sympathy over their father's death, she departed. Tom realised afterwards that she hadn't asked him about his time in prison at all. Perhaps she didn't like to, he thought, out of tact. He was excited at the prospect of her coming up to London and was desperate to see her again.

The funeral took place the next day at the local church and was a simple affair. Tom's mother was quite emotional and he supported her on his arm throughout. All of the family were there, except Dick, and quite few friends. Afterwards, they went back to the cottage for a simple meal and refreshments. The cottage was rented so his mother would now have to move out. She was going to live with Eddie and his wife, and Lizzie was finally going to marry her young man. He had been waiting patiently for over a year, whilst she had helped her father and supported her mother. That night, Tom couldn't sleep and got up to sit by the fire for a while. He found his mother sitting there, silently crying. He held her tight and comforted her as best he could.

"I don't know what to do now," she said. "I have been needed so much and now I'm not. I feel lost. I don't have any purpose anymore!"

Tom tried to cheer her up by reminding her that when she moved in with Eddie she would be needed to help with the children. This did make her feel a bit better, but she said it would take a bit of getting used to, not running her own home.

"Maybe Eddie can find you something special to do," said Tom.

The next day, Tom had a private word with Eddie and explained her feelings. Eddie had an idea about it and later that day, asked their mother whether she could help teach his eldest daughter how to cook and sew. Their mother was only too pleased to be useful, and felt much happier.

That last day before they went back up to London again was spent in helping move Lizzie's and their mother's belongings to their new homes. Lizzie was going to stay with Sarah for a few weeks before she got married. It was a busy day, but late in the afternoon Tom made an excuse and disappeared off. He wanted to see Mary Ann again and went to her home with a bunch of flowers.

"Oh, how sweet!" she said when she saw him at the door, and she invited him in for tea.

Her father was out so they spent a happy couple of hours chatting. Mary Ann had changed, however. She was more sophisticated and liked to tease him. Tom didn't really understand all she said to him, but he was in awe of her. He started to talk about his experiences in prison at one point, but she firmly dismissed all talk of this, saying, "Oh, Tom. None of that. I can't bear to hear it!"

"Well okay," said Tom uncertainly. "But it's a part of my life, all the same."

"It's all in the past now," she said. "Let's not talk about it again."

The subject changed and the slight awkwardness between them disappeared. She regaled Tom with tales of her time in Bristol, making him laugh and gasp alternately.

He left, hoping he would see her again soon in London. He was as much in love with her as ever.

Chapter 12

Shortly after Tom got back from London, Dick's wife Eliza gave birth to their first child, a daughter whom they named Jane. All was not well, however. Unfortunately, the birth went very badly and Eliza was very ill and nearly died. Dick was in a terrible state not knowing what to do for the best. The baby was weak and sickly from the start, and only five days later, the poor little thing died. Meanwhile, Eliza was fighting for her life and somehow pulled through, but the doctors said she would not be able to have any more children. She had been badly damaged internally. Tom felt very sorry for them both. He knew how much Dick had wanted a family. He'd always talked about having a son and heir. Poor Eliza said she felt like a failure, but Dick was a kind and loving husband and did his best to comfort her. He was just glad they were both still together. Even so, privately with Tom, Dick let loose his anger, not at Eliza, but at the world and the universe, who could let this happen.

"You need to get married and have a family," he told Tom. "It's what life is all about. I wish I could. I can't even carry on the Finnimore line!"

Tom promised him he would do his best to oblige, and cheered him up by reminding him that he had a wonderful wife.

"Children aren't everything," Tom said. "We have to accept whatever we're given. You have each other and you're very lucky."

It was the first time Tom had ever seen his brother at a loss. He tried his best to comfort him, but his words seemed trite and meaningless.

A few weeks later, Tom was happy to hear from Will that Mary Ann was coming to visit. He'd been thinking about her day and night since he returned to London, so he was delighted at the news. Her father had agreed to spare her for a few days, but only if she travelled up on the train with someone she knew. As it happened, the young curate of Alphington was coming up for a training course in London that week, so she was able to get him as a chaperone. Will's wife Ann would look after her whilst she was there and Tom would be able to see her every evening. It was summer time so the evenings stayed light until late, and Tom planned to take her walking around the parks and avenues, to show her the nicer side of London. He wasn't sure what she'd make of the streets, so caked with horse dung and mud that you couldn't walk down them without getting covered, so he figured a ride on the new horse drawn omnibus would probably be the best thing. The first evening he went over to Will's and she seemed genuinely delighted to see him.

"Oh, Tom," she said. "I missed you. Life's been so dull down in Devon. Where shall we go?"

That night they walked out through Bermondsey over the beautiful stone arches of London Bridge, over the Thames and up to the Tower of London. She was so excited by the thought of all the drama that had gone on there over the years; the royalty, the treason, the executions.

"There's a rumour they're going to build another bridge over from here to the other side soon," said Tom. "It'd be good if they do, it'll make it a lot quicker to get our goods out into London."

Mary Ann watched the ravens circling overhead and let her imagination soar with them. "Were you in a prison like this?" she asked suddenly.

Tom laughed. "Not quite!" he replied. "I'll show you Millbank one evening this week. You can see what you think."

This he did the very next night, taking her over into Westminster, where she saw the Abbey. They were just starting work on the new Houses of Parliament now and there were workmen everywhere. Mary Ann was fascinated to see the Abbey where the coronation took place. She told Tom she wished she'd seen it.

"I saw the procession," he said. "And I thought I saw you in Hyde Park at the fair."

"It wasn't me," said Mary Ann sadly. "I wasn't able to go."

"I was always thinking about you," said Tom, "and I convinced myself it was you."

"That's so sweet," said Mary Ann. "Did you really think about me?"

"All the time whilst I was in prison," admitted Tom. "It helped keep me going."

"Oh how romantic!" squealed Mary Ann and she took his hand for a brief moment.

This gave him hope for the future. He showed Mary Ann the prison from a distance and her eyes filled with sudden tears.

"Oh, Tom, how awful for you. You were so brave."

"I don't know about that," he muttered, but she refused to believe otherwise, so he let it lie. If she wanted to believe he was strong and brave he wasn't going to argue with her.

The next night, he took her on a horse drawn omnibus up to the Grecian Saloon at the Eagle Tavern. There was a music and supper club there and he thought she would enjoy it. It was a bit rowdy as it was mostly working class and contained a rougher element than he would have liked, but the better establishments cost more, and besides, women were not allowed. He needn't have worried. Mary Ann was thrilled by it and couldn't stop talking about the singers and entertainers all the way home. She seemed easily impressed by London and able to overlook the seedier, dirtier side which was day-to-day reality.

He told Mary Ann about Eliza and Dick's recent misfortune and to his surprise, she burst into tears.

"How sad," she said and was genuinely upset.

Tom felt closer to her, seeing her emotions and he admired her sensitivity.

During the week, they also visited St Paul's Cathedral and The Strand, which Mary Ann found very glamorous and exciting. It came to the final evening and Tom wanted to take her somewhere romantic. They had had a wonderful time together, but only as friends. There was no sign of anything more, but Tom was hopeful. He found her fascinating, lively and as lovely as ever. It was a beautiful evening, and so he decided to take her to Hyde Park to walk along by The Serpentine. They enjoyed a gentle stroll, arm in arm, admiring the late evening sun glinting off the water and the ducks coming in to roost. Tom tried to open up to her about his panic at the Coronation.

"I came here with Lizzie on the day," he said awkwardly. "I needed to get away from the crowds. It was all too much for me."

"Oh, Tom, you idiot!" Mary Ann exclaimed. "They're only people, you know."

Tom felt flustered and embarrassed; she obviously didn't understand.

"It was only 'cos of prison," he stammered.

"Well, I'd have thought you'd be glad to see people again after all that," she said. "You were so lucky to be there and see it all."

"Yes," he agreed. "I suppose I was. We had a really good view from up here and then we all went to the fair. I don't have a problem with crowds now," he added.

"Well, there you are then!" said Mary Ann. "It was just silliness."

"Maybe it was," replied Tom, but he fell silent, feeling a bit hurt.

They sat down on a seat by the water, watching the sun set in a blaze of spectacular colour. Mary Ann realised that she had upset Tom and suddenly turned to him, her eyes concerned and sad.

"I'm sorry," she said. "Sometimes I say too much. You're not an idiot."

Tom felt suddenly emotional and knew he had to tell her his feelings.

"It's okay," he told her. "Look Mary Ann, I've had a wonderful time this week with you, but I'd like to know where I stand. I feel the same as I ever did. What about you?"

"Oh, Tom," she said, her eyes misting over. "I'm very fond of you, but it's too early to tell. I have so many things I want to do – maybe in the future, who knows?"

"You once said you'd wait for me," replied Tom. "Not that I'm holding you to anything, but I hoped you'd still care."

"Tom, we were just children then," said Mary Ann. "We didn't know what we were saying. A lot has changed since then."

They sat there silently, both in their own thoughts, not knowing what to say.

"Let's walk back," said Tom as dusk started coming in. "You don't want to be out here at night."

They parted at Will's house and Tom hoped they could stay in touch.

"I'm coming down to Devon in a few weeks for Lizzie's wedding," he told her. "Maybe I'll see you then."

"I hope so," replied Mary Ann. "I do like you Tom, you must know that. It's just too soon."

He pressed her hand gently, then left, feeling thoroughly miserable.

It was September before Tom came down to Devon for Lizzie's wedding. Leaves were just beginning to change colour and the weather had deteriorated. The London roads were a sea of foul smelling mud. The whole family travelled down together from London by train. Eliza was now on the mend and able to travel, although she still looked pale. It was a very happy gathering that weekend.

In the time since Mary Ann had visited, Tom had received one letter from her, which had been read to him by Will's wife, Ann. It was mostly full of local Alphington news, but she did say that she was looking forward to seeing him again, which raised his hopes a little. He had been desperately sad for the last couple of months. Apparently, Lizzie had invited Mary Ann to the wedding. Tom knew this must be for his sake, since Lizzie barely knew her. The night before the wedding, Tom had a chance to thank her for this.

"It's okay," said Lizzie. "Look Tom, I know you love her and I want you to be happy, but be careful. Mary Ann's had her head turned by the fancy life in Bristol and I'm not sure she'll settle down yet. Although, I have to say, that when I saw her the other day, she asked after you and said to send her fond regards, so I invited her along tomorrow so you could have the chance to be together. Just be careful, that's all."

Tom barely heard her words of warning. He was so happy that Mary Ann was thinking of him and wanting to see him again. He couldn't wait for the next day.

The wedding was a simple country affair at the local church, with Reverend Ellicombe officiating. Lizzie looked beautiful and so happy. Tom was really pleased for her. She was a gentle and kind person who always put others first. Her husband-to-be, Daniel, was a lucky man. Tom saw Mary Ann at the back of the church and he nodded and smiled from a distance. Afterwards, in the churchyard, with rice and petals flying everywhere, they found themselves suddenly together. Mary Ann looked radiant in a beautiful blue gown and Tom had his Sunday suit on, so they made a handsome couple. She seemed a little nervous to see him, but he greeted her so warmly that this soon disappeared. She took his arm and they followed the wedding party back for the celebrations. There was food and wine flowing and music playing, and there seemed to be a certain romance in the air. Tom and Mary Ann stayed together all evening; talking, dancing, laughing. They were inseparable. At the end of the evening, Tom saw Mary Ann out and stood there for a moment, hesitating. He took both her hands in his, saying, "It's been a wonderful evening, Mary Ann."

She looked deep into his eyes and moved closer. "I've enjoyed being with you again, Tom," she said quietly. "I've missed you."

Against all his better judgement then, Tom took her in his arms and kissed her, and she responded in a way which showed she felt the same. They stood close together for a minute or two, then drew apart reluctantly so she could leave.

"I'll write to you," she promised. "I'm trying to find a job in London and then we can spend more time together."

"I'd like that," said Tom and kissed her once more on the cheek as she left. He was so happy he could hardly contain himself.

Chapter 13
November 1842

It wasn't until later that year in November that Mary Ann made the move up to London. Her father was now settled with a housekeeper to look after him, and she had managed to get herself a job at a grand house in Belgravia. Unbeknown to Tom, she had spent her days in London, when she visited before, going around the large houses, leaving her details and references looking for work. This had finally paid off and she was to be employed as a parlour maid. She was very excited at the prospect, and when Tom met her off the train she could talk of nothing else. He was worried that a grand house would turn her head again, and that she wouldn't want to see someone like him from the south side of the river. The south side was the working class poor, working in the industries which kept the city wealthy, but kept the rest of the population in poverty. It was dirty, smoky and smelly, and Tom knew he would have to make extra efforts to wash, using the basic standpipes which were the only opportunity to get clean. However, Mary Ann agreed to spend Sundays with him after church, and also one evening a week, on the day she finished early. Tom was over the moon and planned all sorts of outings for them.

Things started off very well. Tom would clean himself up then call for her at the house. Not that he knocked; he would have been turned away. No, he just waited outside patiently, until she appeared at an agreed time. They tended to go out to supper in the evenings as the winter nights were dark now in spite of the newly installed gas street lighting. London wasn't a safe place to go wandering around in the dark. There were pickpockets and muggers around who would cut your throat as soon as look at you. On Sundays, he tended to take Mary Ann for walks in the park if the weather was nice, or to a tea room if it was wet.

Mary Ann was happy working at the house, impressed with all the grandeur and the fine way of life. She got on well with most of the other servants, and the Master was always very friendly and kind to her. The Mistress was quite haughty and barely spoke. Mary Ann wondered why, but didn't let it bother her. The elderly housekeeper also seemed to disapprove of Mary Ann and made her work very hard. There were often harsh words said and sometimes she was kept late.

The Christmas season arrived and the shops in London were all displaying the new, fancy iced cakes, covered with gilt and decorations, which were the latest fashion. Tom and Mary Ann browsed the brightly lit shop windows during their evening strolls out to supper, and they were amazed by them. They had never seen anything so wonderful, although they were way out of their price range. Mary Ann had to work at Christmas, so Tom spent it with Dick, Eliza, Will, Ann and their happy, healthy, ever increasing brood of children. They had a merry time eating roasted goose and plum porridge. At the New Year, Tom saw Mary Ann again and, as was the tradition at that time, they exchanged small gifts of fruit and nuts. Mary Ann was full of all the excitement of having spent Christmas in a big house and she talked non-stop about the fancy dress, the gifts and the 'role reversal' which saw the servants get to 'rule the roost' for a day. She was delighted with the pretty little trinket boxes which all the female servants had been given by the Master of the house, and Tom felt his small gift of apples couldn't really compare. Nonetheless, they enjoyed their time together. Tom left that night, secretly dreaming of a New Year spent with Mary Ann, and hoping it would come true.

A few weeks went by and Tom was seeing Mary Ann regularly, however, he felt she was becoming more distant from him. They had exchanged kisses and embraces and he had told her that he loved her, but she had still not committed herself to him. She often teased him and was flirtatious, leading him on, then leaving him high and dry. He didn't really know how she felt about him. He knew she didn't really approve of his job and he felt this could be a barrier between them. He was still working for Jim and enjoying it, but was thinking of maybe breaking out on his own as a journeyman tanner, someone who travelled around different places, bringing their experience to others. He felt this might be a step that Mary Ann would approve of, and that maybe she would agree to marry him.

Meanwhile, Mary Ann was becoming more and more taken with the Belgravia way of life. There were grand parties and balls, and although she was just a servant, she got to see it all. One day, she told Tom how the Master was always seeking her out and giving her extra treats and little presents. This made Tom feel both jealous and anxious. Surely a grand man like her Master would not be interested in a country girl? Or maybe he would, but for just one thing. Tom warned Mary Ann to take care as it may be that her Master had designs on her, but Mary Ann flew into a rage at him.

"How dare you suggest such a thing?" she cried. Her eyes flashed with temper. "He likes me and respects me, and besides, you should know I'm not that kind of girl!"

"*I* know you're not," said Tom trying to pacify her. "But *he* may not. Just be careful, that's all."

"I can take care of myself, thank you!" she retorted. "I don't need your lectures." Then she stormed out, and although Tom called after her, she refused to listen.

A week passed and Tom went to the house twice as usual, but Mary Ann didn't come out. He waited an hour and a half, then went, slowly and sadly, back to his small flat. He shouldn't have said anything, he thought. Now he'd wrecked everything between them. He tried again the following week, but it was still the same. He thought he saw a curtain move in an upstairs window, but no one appeared. Maybe he could get Will's wife, Ann to write to her for him, he thought; but what could he say? As it happened, there was no need, for the following evening there was a knock at his door and Mary Ann stood there in floods of tears. Her dress was torn at the shoulder and her arms were bruised. She had her bags with her. She fell sobbing into his arms and told him the whole sorry story. It seemed the Master, unfortunately, did indeed have designs on her and having followed her into a linen cupboard, attempted to put them into practice. She refused and a struggle broke out, hence the torn dress and bruises. His Lordship, for such he was, called her a filthy whore and told her to leave the house immediately. Mary Ann went to the Mistress in tears to ask for her help, but her Ladyship just laughed in her face.

"What did you think would happen?" she said. "If you tease a man like that, you have to expect it. Most of the maids are happy enough with the attention. You're just a little flirt – all talk and no action. Get out!"

Mary Ann collected her things and went downstairs, telling the housekeeper she was leaving on the way out. Surprisingly, the older woman spoke quite kindly to her.

"Get outta here while you still can, dearie. Get yourself a decent young man, like that one who's been hanging around all the time. Don't waste yer time with the likes of these lot. They may be rich, but they ain't decent. There's been a lot of girls who got into trouble since they been 'ere, if you know what I mean! I'm glad to see you got more sense."

Mary Ann hugged her suddenly and then left.

Tom spent some time comforting her and calming her down.

When she finally stopped crying, she muttered, "I don't know what to do now. I've no job and no home. I'll have to go back to Devon. I won't be able to get another job here. They won't give me a reference. I'm sorry I didn't listen to you, Tom. I was wrong!"

Tom kissed her again and said, "The best thing you can do Mary Ann, is to stay here and marry me. You know I love you and I can offer you a home and a stable income. I was thinking of going self-employed and moving further out from here. We could make a good life together, Mary Ann. Will you be my wife, *please*?"

"Do you mean it?" she asked tearfully. "Do you really want to marry me?"

"More than anything else in the world!" replied Tom. "If you feel you could care for me, that is."

"Care for you? I love you, Tom! Of course I'll be your wife. Nothing would make me happier!" They embraced passionately and Tom realised this was the happiest day of his life so far.

Chapter 14

Tom reflected that a lot could happen in a year. This time last year, he was about to attend his father's funeral, completely unaware that he would ever see Mary Ann again. Now he was going to marry her! It's funny how things can change, he thought.

They got married on 1st April 1843. Some people said it was strange getting married on April Fool's Day, but Tom just laughed and said he'd be a fool not to. Mary Ann insisted they get married in London, as she didn't want a 'country' wedding. Tom was a bit disappointed not to be getting married in Alphington, but went along with it to please her. The wedding was to take place in the Holy Trinity church, Clapham and most of the family hoped to get there in spite of the distance. They had managed to find a small terraced house in Clapham, not far from the Common, to live in when they were married. Clapham was quite an affluent area, and had had some very famous people living there recently, like William Wilberforce, the great social reformer. There were many grand houses built directly around the Common. Mary Ann was very impressed by being in the heart of all this grandeur and she was very keen to make their home there. Tom was a little worried about the cost of the rent, but thought as long as Mary Ann was careful with the housekeeping, they'd be alright. With a few negotiations, Tom had managed to get some contracts for work in the future and he was very hopeful. He parted with Jim on good terms and knew he could always go back there if he needed to, although Mary Ann was dead set against it.

"You don't need to work in any smelly old tannery now!" she declared. "You're a craftsman and can earn your own living. Besides, being out by the Common is a good place to bring up children."

She smiled and kissed him and he was only too happy to agree.

The day of the wedding came at last. Mary Ann had been keen to follow the latest fashion, as set by Queen Victoria at her own wedding, of getting married in white. The royal wedding had been a grand affair in February 1840 and many new fashions in bridal wear were started at that time. Tom remembered the day fondly, as they'd all had a holiday from work, but to be honest, he hadn't taken much notice of what the Queen was wearing. There were huge crowds everywhere again, which he avoided as much as possible. St James' Park and the route from Buckingham Palace to St James' Palace were unbearable for him, but he sheltered from the heavy rain in a local alehouse with his brothers, Dick and Will, for much of the time. (Their wives had gone off to join the crowds). There were the usual heralds, trumpets, carriages and processions, but they happily let most of it pass them by.

White dresses, like the Queen's, were too expensive however, and despite Mary Ann's pleadings and tears to her father and to Tom, she had to be satisfied with having a pale blue silk day dress for the occasion. Tom just wore his best suit; they hadn't got the money to start paying out for new clothes for him as well. They did manage to get Mary Ann some beautiful white flowers for her bouquet and a lace veil, so in the end she was quite happy and certainly looked very beautiful on the day. All the family on both sides also did their best to contribute to the wedding breakfast, so this helped. The Holy Trinity church was an elegant brick building right by the Common, with a short tower, a clock and even four church bells. Tom arranged for the bells to be rung as they left at the end of the ceremony, which delighted Mary Ann. It cost extra, but he wanted so much to please her.

It was a simple but meaningful service, surrounded by most of their families. Tom was sure and steady in his responses to the vicar, Mary Ann a little more nervous. The party afterwards at the local parish hall was a very happy one. The happy couple drank and danced until late, then went back to their new house for the wedding night. Tom was nervous about the nuptials. He wasn't sure how Mary Ann would react and he didn't want to hurt her. He needn't have worried; she was passionate and giving, holding nothing back. Tom, in return, was gentle and loving. Afterwards, they lay in each other's arms, enjoying the afterglow of their lovemaking. Mary Ann's eyes were shining brightly with tears of joy and Tom wished he could stay like that forever. It had been almost a spiritual experience.

Day to day life couldn't be kept away for long however, and they started their new life together as husband and wife. Tom worked hard and Mary Ann kept the house. She was proud of their sparklingly clean home and the high standard of her cooking. There were always flowers on the table and the best china for dinner. Tom loved coming home to her after a hard day's work. They spent their evenings cuddled up together by the fire and Sundays walking on the Common. The first few months of married life were delightful. Mary Ann always managed to look beautiful and often seemed to have a new dress that he hadn't seen before, or a new hairstyle. He wondered how she managed it all. The meals were much better than he was used to and he marvelled at how she made the money go so far. On one or two occasions, she asked him for extra, but he was giving her all his wages already, so had none to spare. Then one day, he came home and found her in tears.

"What's wrong?" he asked.

"The horrid baker's man has sent in a huge bill," she wailed. "And you don't give me enough money to pay for it, so I don't know what to do!"

Tom was worried – there should have been enough money. What had happened to it all? When he looked into it further, he was horrified to find other unpaid bills lying around. He questioned Mary Ann about it and she quickly got upset, crying, "It's not my fault. You don't give me enough housekeeping."

Tom got angry now for the first time ever with Mary Ann. "I've given you enough, but now I find you've spent it on dresses and fripperies. It's got to stop, Mary Ann!"

They argued bitterly, with Mary Ann crying and Tom angry. He was annoyed because he thought she'd been making ends meet. He'd trusted her and she'd let him down but, he reasoned, she was young and inexperienced as a housekeeper, so he had to make some allowances. Later that evening, he sat down and spoke to her calmly and kindly about the situation.

"Look Mary Ann, we need to get this sorted out and then everything will be okay again. Let's deal with the urgent bills and send back the things we haven't used yet. It's not your fault. You did your best; I should have been more involved. Unfortunately, we can't live this way, it's beyond our means. We've got to cut down."

Tearfully she agreed, and they sorted out the bills and satisfied the creditors. Mary Ann did throw a tantrum when Tom said a bale of fine cotton designated for a new dress would have to be sent back as well, but he put his foot down and she gave in. He was pleased that she had seen sense.

Life returned to normal, although Tom tried to keep a closer eye on the finances in future. Mostly they had a happy time together. Life was never dull with Mary Ann around. Her emotions were always up and down, but she was a passionate and loving wife. Before long, however, another drain on their income arrived. Mary Ann was pregnant with their first child. They were both delighted and Tom did everything he could to ease things for Mary Ann. She wanted to have a woman come to the house to clean for her whilst she was pregnant, but Tom refused due to lack of money, and did his best to help out in the evenings himself. He also asked his sister in law, Eliza, whether she would help out, which she was only too happy to do. She was glad to be involved, despite not being able to have children of her own. Mary Ann wanted all sorts of things for the forthcoming baby, and although Will's wife Ann was happy to provide them second-hand, Mary Ann said these simply wouldn't do, and unknown to Tom, went out and bought them new. Money slipped through her fingers like water through a sieve. The bills began to mount up again, but Tom felt he couldn't refuse Mary Ann things for their firstborn child. She shed many tears when he suggested taking the 'hand me downs' and she convinced him that they would be covered in germs and dirt and not fit for their forthcoming arrival. So he took on some extra work, which meant working longer hours and staying away overnight. He didn't want to, as he missed her so much, but, he thought, it would be worth it if they got the things they needed. Mary Ann was desolate with him away and so happy to see him when he came home. They were hardly sleeping together at all at the moment, what with Mary Ann being pregnant. She said she didn't feel right about it. Tom was very understanding. He cared about her and the unborn baby's health and didn't want to put them at risk.

The day of the birth was both nerve wracking and wonderful for Tom. The midwife was there and Tom wasn't allowed anywhere near until after the baby arrived. He heard Mary Ann screaming in the distance and was desperately worried. Would she be okay? Was the baby alright? His fears were put to rest at 9 o' clock that evening when he was able to see his newborn daughter for the first time. The sight of the baby moved him so much that he felt tears come to his eyes. He loved the little girl unconditionally from the start. He knelt by Mary Ann's bed, telling her how proud he was of her and how much he loved her.

"What are we going to call her?" he said.

"Why Mary, of course," she replied.

"Why not another name like Elizabeth or Ann?" he asked. "We'll just get confused if there's two 'Marys' in the house."

She was insistent however, and Tom knew he would never get her to change her mind. When she was like this, there was no shifting her.

Little Mary was a healthy, happy baby who caused little trouble. To save confusion she came to be known as Molly, which Tom preferred. She smiled a lot and chuckled prettily at Tom when he amused her with her rattle. He adored her. He would have liked to help more with the baby, but Mary Ann said he was being silly, it was women's work. As the baby grew, Mary Ann would proudly take her out in the pram for walks around the Common. She loved to dress her up in pretty lace dresses to show her off, so Tom worked harder than ever to try to get the things they needed. He was beginning to wonder if they could afford to stay in Clapham long term.

Molly was approaching her second birthday when Mary Ann announced she was expecting again. Tom was pleased, but worried how they would make ends meet. This time, he insisted they take advantage of the second hand items freely offered by his family. They could also re-use some of the things they had had for the first baby. Mary Ann was not happy about any of this, but Tom managed to convince her. He suggested that if they didn't, they may have to move to a cheaper area, which she certainly didn't want to do.

John (named after Mary Ann's father) was born in 1846, just around the time Tom turned thirty. He was a sickly child for a while, although he picked up slowly and steadily. During this time, Mary Ann spent a lot of money on things for him, and she accused Tom of causing the baby's weakness by having second hand things for him. Tom had to go away again for work for a few days in order to make some extra money. When he came back, he was horrified to find Mary Ann had been busy spending money for herself and the baby, whilst he was away. Tom was furious. "What did you do that for? You know we can't afford it!"

"But you've been earning extra, anyway," she argued. "And I was so bored while you were away that I had to do something. We need these things!"

Reluctantly, Tom had to make her send most of them back and Mary Ann refused to speak to him for several days. They sat at the dinner table together, eating but not talking. He could hardly look her in the face. Eventually, they only started talking again when little Molly, who was starting to toddle about, fell over and hurt herself. They both rushed over to her side and in the natural process of looking after her, found themselves communicating normally again.

Chapter 15

Time went by but things didn't get any easier. Tom often had to be away for a few days at a time in order to bring in enough money for them all, and he felt he was missing out on his children growing up. Mary Ann almost seemed to approve of him being away now, as the extra money was always useful. Their time together was less and Mary Ann was always too tired, from looking after the children she said, to make love. Any intimacy had ceased between them. In fact, when Tom tried to kiss her when he came back from one of his trips away, she recoiled from him, saying, "Tom, you smell awful! Go and clean yourself up. You're disgusting!"

Tom missed the sense of closeness they had had. Mary Ann seemed only interested in living a fine life and spending money. She spoilt the children and was living well above their means.

It all came to a head one day in 1848 when Tom came home to find her entertaining a group of young mothers and babies at their house. He said 'hello' politely, but they just looked at him as if he was something alien. After they'd gone, he asked Mary Ann why they'd been there and what they'd been eating.

"We'd been having a dress fitting," she said. "And then I asked them back afterwards to keep me company. I get so bored and lonely; you're never here, so I have to have someone to talk to. We had tea and cake, if you must know!"

Dresses! Cake! What was she spending now? Tom saw red and marched into the kitchen and started going through the drawers. He pulled out handfuls of unpaid bills from different places and was shocked to see some letters demanding final payment or further action would be taken. One or two of them were very threatening indeed.

"Mary Ann!" he exclaimed. "What's going on? These need to be paid. Where's all the money?"

"All what money? There's never enough!" she cried. "You leave me short all the time. You're so mean."

"Right. That's it!" Tom blurted out angrily. "We're leaving Clapham now and moving back to Bermondsey. It's a lot cheaper and we can stay with Dick and Eliza for a while till we get sorted out. We're just going to end up in debtor's prison if we stay here."

"Oh well, you'd know all about prison, wouldn't you?" she retorted. "That's why you can't earn a good living – because you're an ex-con! I'm not moving back to Bermondsey. You can forget that idea. There's cholera there. You can't expect us to put up with that. You're cruel and heartless!"

"Mary Ann," said Tom, trying to stay calm. "Please listen. Okay, maybe not Bermondsey, but we've got to leave here. We can't afford it. You're spending too much."

"If you can't keep us properly, Tom, then I'm leaving! I'll go to my sister in Bristol and I'm taking the children with me."

"Please!" cried Tom. "Mary Ann – you and the children mean everything to me. Don't leave! Let's work this out."

"Forget it! If you cared, you'd provide for us. I should never have married you." With that she stormed out of the room, took the children and locked herself into the bedroom, crying.

Tom and Mary Ann did not speak for many days. He had to sleep downstairs and make his own meals, whilst she remained apart with the children upstairs. Molly was crying for Papa; he heard her in the evenings and it made his heartache, but Mary Ann refused to come down unless he was out at work. She wrote to her sister Hannah in Bristol, but was not able to go there as she had just given birth to her fifth child and they had no room. So Mary Ann arranged to go back to her father in Devon. Tom, meanwhile, gave notice on the house and spent time settling debts and returning, or selling, goods. He very sadly sold most of their furniture. He knew now that their marriage was probably over. His heart felt broken, but he realised now what Mary Ann was really like. She was extravagant, selfish and even a bully at times. He still loved her but wasn't sure he could live with her any more. However, he had to try for the sake of the children. The thought that she was taking his children away made him feel desperately sad, but he knew he couldn't look after them on his own, so what could he do? He tried reasoning with her through the bedroom door, but she just told him to go away. He told her what he had done with the house and that they needed to be out by the end of the month. Then he begged her to give things another try and told her he still loved her, but there was no reply.

The end of the month came and Tom packed up what things he had left. On the final day, Mary Ann and the children left the confines of the bedroom. Men were coming later that day to remove their marriage bed, which Tom had also had to sell. He had just about managed to pay everything off in the nick of time. A couple more weeks and they would have been summoned for their debts. His plans were to stay with his brother for a while, unless Mary Ann relented. When she appeared he could see she'd been crying, which gave him hope.

"Mary Ann," he appealed, "please listen to reason. We need to be together as a family. I still love you and want to be with you. What's more, I love my children. They need their father. Please!"

As if to back up what he was saying, little Molly, who was now four years old, ran to him and hugged his legs, saying, "Papa."

His son, John, was only two and so barely noticed what was going on. Mary Ann held his small hand tightly.

Tom picked up Molly and hugged her tight, saying, "Papa loves you Molly. Remember that."

He felt himself welling up with emotion. Mary Ann looked at him coldly.

"It's over, Tom," she said firmly. "You can't give me the life I want and that our children deserve. I'm not going back to those rat infested slums where your brother lives. It's not fair to ask it. We'll all end up in some workhouse, or dead from some awful disease!"

"Why don't I come down to Devon with you?" Tom asked pleadingly. "I could find work there. We could start again."

"I don't want you there, Tom. I've been thinking about it a lot in the last couple of weeks, and I realise I don't love you anymore. I'm sorry, but you've let me down badly!"

"I've let *you* down?" cried Tom. "I like that!" He stopped himself, but Mary Ann picked it up again.

"See!" she said angrily. "It won't work, Tom. Keep away from us. We don't want you anymore!"

With that she snatched Molly out of his arms, even though the little girl started screaming, then she headed out the front door. A horse and cart had just arrived to pick them up. All their belongings were loaded on, while Tom stood there helplessly.

"Can I at least come and visit the children?" he asked. "I love them. They're mine as well."

"Please yourself," cried Mary Ann, "but you won't be welcomed!"

They climbed onto the cart and it drove away, little Molly still crying and John looking scared. Tom stood gazing after them, his heart in pieces. It was the end of his dreams. His world was shattered.

Chapter 16

Tom packed up the last of his belongings and gave them to the carrier to take to Dick and Eliza's house. He had a last wander around their empty house, gazing sadly at the bedroom where they used to lie together. In the kitchen he gathered up his small bag of immediate clothing and supplies, but was caught suddenly by the sight of a child's small woollen sock on the floor. He picked it up sorrowfully and put it in his bag as well – a small souvenir of happier times. Then he locked the house and left it for good. After handing the keys in to the landlady, he went to the local alehouse and drank the cheapest, roughest ale all night to try and blot out the pain. He woke up the next morning on a park bench on the Common. His head throbbed and his eyes hurt with the morning light. How did he get here? He didn't know. He was stiff and cold, so he stood up to try and straighten out, but felt so dizzy he could hardly stand. His mouth felt like sawdust; he needed water. After a cheap breakfast at a local tearoom he felt a bit better. He looked across the Common, past the grand stately homes, and saw their little terraced house in the distance. He couldn't stay around here – he knew that. He headed out of Clapham and never went back.

What happened in the next week, he never fully remembered. He vaguely recollected wandering in a daze from place to place, eating occasionally and drinking often. He sometimes woke up under a hedge and once in a ditch. He didn't care. Finally, he stood by the Thames and contemplated jumping in. It would make no difference to anyone, he thought. Mary Ann and the children didn't want him. He had no home, no wife, no children and no fixed job. What did it matter if he existed or not? The only reason he didn't do it was because he passed out from hunger and fatigue and came to a while later to see an old woman peering anxiously at him. Her face was wrinkled with age but her eyes were kind and wise.

"You alright, young man?" she asked. "You look about done in. Do you need a place to stay?"

Tom tried to mutter 'no, I don't want anything', but she wouldn't listen. She helped him to his feet and took him to a humble looking cottage nearby.

"'Ere love," she said, giving him a mug of warm tea. "Get that down you. You'll feel better for it."

Tom did as he was told and started to revive. The old woman told him her name was Ellen, but everyone called her 'Old Nellie'. She lived alone, her husband dead and her children left home. She fed him and made up a bed for him. Tom was hardly able to speak, but murmured his thanks as he fell asleep.

"That's alright, dearie, you get yer rest."

The next day, he awoke feeling refreshed and was able to tell her his troubles. He felt he could speak to her without being judged. The kindness of a stranger had saved him.

"So what you gonna do then?" she asked.

"I'm going to go to my brother first," replied Tom. "Then see what happens. You've been so kind, I must find a way to thank you."

"Oh go on with you!" she said. "Get off to your brother and don't be so bloody daft in future. No silly little fool of a girl like her is worth it. You're better off without 'er!"

Tom couldn't agree at present but he pulled himself together, thanked her again then headed straight over to Dick and Eliza's house. They were very relieved to see him, as the carrier had delivered his things a week ago and they were worried he hadn't turned up soon after. He didn't stay with them for long however. He couldn't bear their sympathy, no matter how well meaning it was. He headed off into Surrey to find work. Maybe he could have gone back to work for Jim again, but he felt like it was going backwards. He needed to be alone, and so over the next few months he went from place to place, a few days or weeks here and there, working in a variety of different tanning yards.

Tom worked long hours without caring, his work mechanical but thorough. All he wanted at the end of each day was to be able to fall asleep from sheer exhaustion and blot out the memories. He didn't care about his appearance or his own welfare. He spoke no more than he had to, not socialising with anyone. He ate and slept wherever he could, either at the workplace or in the cheapest, most basic lodgings available. People saw him as surly and morose. Those who tried to engage him in conversation were cut short and therefore didn't bother any more. He soon got a reputation for being a good worker but a poor workmate. Nobody understood that he didn't dare let any feelings show, otherwise he might crack. Tom tried not to think about anything, but after a few months, it suddenly occurred to him that little Molly's fifth birthday was fast approaching. He wished he hadn't remembered because as soon as he had, he couldn't get it out of his mind. He'd heard from Lizzie that Mary Ann and the children had arrived safely in Alphington and were living with her father. Maybe he should go down and see them, if only to give Molly a birthday present? He wasn't sure what to give her, but he decided on a small doll from the local shop. The shopkeeper looked at him suspiciously – a dirty, unshaven, rough-looking man, buying toys for children. She pursed her lips but reluctantly sold him what he wanted. Tom noticed the look of disapproval and felt annoyed, but when he caught sight of his reflection in the shop window, he could see her point. If he was going to visit his estranged family, he would have to clean himself up.

After a visit to the local bath-house, he headed off on the train to Devon. He felt very nervous but decided it was the right thing to do. His children deserved the attention of their father, even if their mother didn't want him anymore. He knocked loudly and was surprised to see Mary Ann's father come to the door. He had thought he would be at work, but apparently not.

"What do you want?" his father in law demanded abruptly. "We don't want you 'round here!"

"I'm here to see my daughter," replied Tom. "I've got a present for her."

"Oh, so now you spend money on her! Before you couldn't even let them have enough for food and clothing. I've heard all about how you treated my daughter – keeping her in poverty all the time, when you had money to spare. Not giving her enough to pay the bills."

"That's not true!" exclaimed Tom. "I gave her money, but she spent it all. I *want* to see my daughter."

His father in law turned back into the house and called, "Mary Ann – your no good husband's here!"

He then disappeared into the cottage, leaving Tom to face Mary Ann. She appeared with the children, one on either hand, but her face was cold and hard.

"You've got a nerve!" she said. "What do you want?"

"I came to give Molly her birthday present," he replied. "Here you are darling. Papa's got something for you."

But six months is a long time in a young child's life and little Molly shrank away from him, clinging to her mother in fear.

"Molly," coaxed Tom. "It's Papa, don't you remember me?"

He moved towards her, but the little girl hid behind Mary Ann. Young John stared at him suspiciously.

"John," Tom said, "it's your papa. I've missed you both."

He held out his hands towards him, but John dropped his mother's hand and ran off into the house, screaming.

"Now see what you've done!" Mary Ann cried. "They don't know you any more, Tom. You're frightening them."

At this point, young Molly seemed to have some memory of him and moved out towards him. "Papa," she said hesitantly.

"Yes, that's right, darling," Tom replied, pleased that she was recognising him again. "I've got something for you. Look."

He handed her the doll, which she took from him, but Mary Ann snatched it away, saying, "You don't want that dirty old thing Molly. You'll catch germs from it."

His daughter started crying and Tom wanted to pick her up and take her away, but Mary Ann held her hand firmly to stop her going to him.

"It's too late, Tom," she said. "Go away. You've upset everyone now. Can't you see? Leave us alone!"

With that she shut the door in Tom's face, and he left broken hearted.

Chapter 17

It was 1851, and Tom was still working his way around Surrey as a tanner, working hard but keeping himself to himself. He had no friends and rarely even saw his family. He had become a loner, just existing from day to day. He tried hard to make out that his work was his life, but that wasn't quite true. Last year, he had heard that Mary Ann's father had died, and unsurprisingly, the household debts were such that they all had to move out. Lizzie told Tom, via letter, that she'd heard that Mary Ann was living at a big farmhouse in Alphington, called Sobey's Farm. She was working there as a laundress. Tom worried about the children's welfare and wondered if he should help out. He'd had no contact with them in two years, but he decided to send some money to her at the address Lizzie had given him. He waited, but heard nothing back. It was the year of the Great Exhibition and Tom kept thinking about how much Mary Ann would have loved to go. All the fancy things and new inventions would have appealed to her. He wondered to himself if maybe she would let him take her and the children to it, just as friends. Then he could make sure they were alright and help out if need be.

One morning, he turned up at Sobey's Farm and was impressed by the size of it. There were many people living and working there, and he figured she was probably just one of the many servants. He asked to see her and an old woman took him down some corridors and into the wash-house. Mary Ann was there, but Tom was surprised by her appearance. She had put on quite a lot of weight and no longer looked so fine. Her hair was scruffy and her clothes shabby, her hands red from washing and scrubbing.

"Mary Ann!" he called. "How are you?"

She looked up surprised to see him and, it seemed to him, embarrassed.

"Tom," she said awkwardly and faltered.

"I wanted to make sure you were okay," he said. "I was sorry to hear about your father."

Then he told her that he had been thinking of them and wondering if they'd like a trip to London to see the Great Exhibition.

"Just as friends," he added. "Nothing more. I know you'd love it."

For a moment, her face lit up with excitement at the thought of it but then she looked away.

"It's good of you Tom, but I can't. I need to stay here, and the children are in school."

Her tone had altered and softened since the last time he had seen her. She was more amenable now, but still out of reach.

"Surely it wouldn't hurt if they missed a bit of school," he reasoned, but just as he said this a large, burly looking man appeared, put his arm proprietarily around Mary Ann's shoulders and said, "This chap bothering you, maid?"

"No, he's okay, Bert," she muttered, embarrassed.

"You want to leave her alone, if you know what's good for you, mate! She's with me." Then he moved off a short distance, but stood watching them.

"I see," said Tom, coldly. "So that's how it is!"

"I'm sorry," replied Mary Ann, her face crimson with shame. "Bert's taking care of me and the kids now, Tom."

"*I* could take care of you!" he protested. "They're *my* children, after all. I sent you some money. Did you get it?"

"Yes, thank you, Tom, but don't send any more. Bert's a good man and he looks after us well. It's been a long while since we two were together and things have changed. It's time to move on, you know."

Tom just gazed at her in silence for a few moments, then turned and walked away. Mary Ann followed after him. By the front door, he turned to her and, more kindly than he felt, said quietly, "If you ever need anything, Mary Ann, you or the children, let me know and I'll do my best to help. My brother Dick in Bermondsey always knows where to reach me."

She started to thank him, but just then Bert appeared again, saying, "I think it's time you cleared off, mate! I don't want you upsetting my missus."

Tom touched her hand briefly then left the house promptly.

Tom realised one thing as he walked down the lane away from the farmhouse; Mary Ann was right. It *was* time to move on. Thinking about the last three years, he suddenly felt ashamed about how distant he had been from his family. They'd all tried to help but he hadn't been able to take their pity, so he subconsciously avoided them. He hadn't been fair, but he couldn't help it. It was just something he had had to go through alone. Now he knew he had to reconnect with them. He started that very afternoon by visiting them all. They were delighted to see him, especially his mother. He ended up in the evening at Lizzie and Daniel's house and they insisted he stay for the night, or longer if he wished. In the course of things, they all got to talking about the much-rumoured 'Great Exhibition' in London.

"I've heard it's an amazing building," said Lizzie. "All made of glass."

"I wanted to take Mary Ann," Tom sighed. "But that's not going to happen."

"I'd have loved to have gone," Lizzie said wistfully. "But the children are too young."

"You could come with me!" suggested Tom enthusiastically. "They're running special, cheap excursion trains and it only costs a shilling to go in, if you go on a week day. I still want to go. I've heard it's wonderful. We could have a great time!"

"I can't, Tom," replied Lizzie. "Who's going to look after Daniel here and the children?"

"Oh yes, I'm sorry," said Tom. "I wasn't thinking. It was a silly idea."

At this point Daniel interjected, "Well, I think it's a great idea! Lizzie, darling, you deserve a few days away. Why don't we see if your mother could come over and help out here for a few days? I'm sure she'd be only too happy, or failing that, maybe Sarah would help."

So it was that Tom and Lizzie made their way to London Hyde Park for the Great Exhibition of the Works of Industry of All Nations. The sight of the enormous glasshouse (known as the 'Crystal Palace') glittering in the sun was spectacular. There were brightly coloured flags of all the nations flying from the roof. Inside, it was dazzling and if it hadn't been for some calico shading, they would have found it far too bright. The exhibition was, naturally, very busy. This brought back memories to Tom of how Lizzie had looked after him at Hyde Park, long ago, and he remarked as much.

"You've always been there for me, Lizzie," he said. "And I'm grateful. I don't know what I'd have done without you that day."

Lizzie just smiled and squeezed his arm.

"You're my brother, Tom," she replied. "Any sister would do the same."

They had a wonderful time. When they got to the very centre of the 'palace' they were able to admire the crystal fountain, which rose many feet into the air. They sat by it and had refreshments of soft drinks and bath buns. They were amazed to see the fully grown Elm trees, which were a natural part of the park, encased inside the building. It had been deliberately built high enough to incorporate them. There was music playing from a pipe organ, and coloured banners everywhere telling them what to see. There were goods and materials from every corner of the world, from exotic silks from India, to fine art from France, to steam engines from Britain. Tom noticed there was even a leather making section and he proudly pointed it out to Lizzie. They enjoyed themselves, trying free samples of different products and seeing the many, fully working items of machinery. There was pottery, porcelain, furniture, fabrics, art, musical instruments, engines, perfume – in fact, almost anything you could think of. Much of it was British or from the Colonies and, as Lizzie said, it gave a marvellous picture of what Britain could achieve. There was even that most recent (and currently rare!) invention – working public lavatories! All in all, it was a memorable experience, and Tom felt pleased that he'd been able to give something nice back to dearest Lizzie for a change.

Chapter 18

It was early 1854, and Tom had just received disturbing news from Devon. For one thing, Lizzie wrote to say there had been bread riots locally, which started in St Thomas in Exeter, but spread down into Alphington. Baker's shop windows were smashed and goods taken, but no one was hurt, thank goodness. (Luckily their brother, John's, fishmonger's shop had escaped unscathed). Some people claimed it all happened because the locals were starving, but others reckoned they were just making trouble. Lizzie said she had seen the rioters from a distance, but stayed well out the way. This was just as well, as most of them ended up getting arrested.

The more disturbing thing, from Tom's point of view, was that Mary Ann and the children had apparently left Alphington with Bert, and no one was sure where they'd gone. Tom had his suspicions that she might have gone to her sister in Bristol, but wished he knew for sure.

He continued working around the Surrey area as a tanner. Work was plentiful, but he never settled anywhere for long. These days he had mellowed a bit and was more friendly and polite to his fellow workers, if still a bit distant. He didn't socialise with them after hours; he preferred his own company on the whole. He did now spend more time with his family, and was happy that he had managed to connect with them again, before it was too late. He usually spent Christmas with one or other of them, and often visited them on a Sunday afternoon.

1854 also brought the sad news of their mother's death, which gathered them all together in a sorrowful farewell in Alphington. She was well into her mid-sixties and had been very frail recently, so it was no surprise, but a great loss none the less. The two people who had brought them into being, and had been the heads of their family, were no longer with them, and they all felt lost. While they stood at the graveside, listening to the vicar's sermon, Tom's mind went back to the night before his trial, all those years ago. He remembered his mother telling him she would always love him, no matter what happened. They had been very close and he knew he would miss her deeply. She'd been a truly wonderful mother to them all – kind, loving, fair-minded and loyal – all the things a mother should be.

Almost all of Tom's siblings were now settled down, married and happy, mostly with children of their own. He seemed to be one of the only ones who weren't, although in name he was still married to Mary Ann and had children somewhere. He guessed they wouldn't even recognise their father now, if they saw him, and he realised he wouldn't know them either. It was a pitiful situation, but he had to accept it. It was unlikely to change.

He also wished his children had known their grandmother, but it was too late now. They might well have passed by each other in the streets of Alphington without the children even knowing it. He doubted his mother would have recognised Mary Ann after not having seen her for several years, and he was certain Mary Ann would have taken pains to avoid any of his family, if she possibly could. Lizzie said she had seen them occasionally in passing before they moved away, but Mary Ann had deliberately snubbed her. It was a sad state of affairs.

Tom returned to London in a sombre mood. He was helping his old boss Jim out for a while at the moment while he was short-handed, and was lodging with Dick and Eliza. However, it suddenly occurred to him that he was back in the same situation he'd been in seventeen years ago. Nothing had changed, he thought to himself, except maybe for the worse. He had no parents now, an absent wife and children, and the same job and lodgings as before. He had nothing against Jim or his brother, but he felt like he was stuck. His career, if it could be called as much, seemed stale. He was going nowhere, he thought. Most of the last few years had been spent moving around from place to place and he realised he was searching for something, but what?

It was at this point he started to seriously consider taking 'the Queen's shilling' and joining up with the troops to go to the Crimean War. At that time, public enthusiasm for the war was high and he'd heard that the soldiers were paid handsomely and treated well. Tom thought long and hard about it. He was not a fighting man and had no appetite for war, but he asked himself: 'Why not be a hero? Why not do your bit for your country? What have you got to lose? Maybe this is what you're searching for.' He knew his mother would have hated the thought of him going, but she wasn't around anymore. He tried to push thoughts of his sister Lizzie to the back of his mind as well; he knew she wouldn't approve. The idea went around and around his head, keeping him awake at night, trying to make the decision. He tried to picture himself killing another man and found it almost impossible to imagine. Why would he want to hurt someone he didn't know, just because he came from a different place to himself? Then again, if it was a matter of survival, he guessed you did what you had to. Perhaps it was right and proper when you were defending your country? He couldn't decide.

Weeks went by and he had almost convinced himself, and was planning to go to a recruitment office on the following Monday morning. That Sunday afternoon, in late October, he spent with Will, Ann and their family. Ann often read the newspaper stories to them as neither Tom nor his brother were very good at reading. This time he was shocked to hear Ann read out the reports of the charge of the Light Brigade and the losses sustained on the British side:

"The charge of the Light Brigade…though brilliantly and bravely done, was most disastrous in its consequences to that gallant and devoted band, for it seems that out of 700 who went into the fray only 130 answered their roll when it was over."

The reporter went on to describe the atrocious conditions of the soldiers, including the disease, the army mismanagement, the fatal blunders and the dreadful injuries sustained. Tom reached the conclusion from this, that the war was nothing but a sad waste of life for little purpose, except to please the people in power. The sacrifice of the ordinary soldier from the working classes meant nothing to them. Tom rapidly came to his senses and decided that a safe, but boring life was preferable to no life at all! He went back to the tannery the following morning with a greater acceptance and a feeling of calm. He vowed he would never be stupid enough to consider such a thing again.

Chapter 19
1858

It was the summer of 1858, and Tom and Mary Ann had been separated for nearly ten years. Tom was in his early forties now and had moved on with his life. He rarely thought about Mary Ann these days, but when he did, there was no bitterness. Mostly he just pitied her. Unfortunately, she had never managed to find what she really wanted from life. His main regret and concern was for the children. He hoped they were okay, but he didn't know where to start looking for them. He didn't even have Hannah's address, (although he knew she lived south of the river in Bristol) so he couldn't contact them if he wanted to. After his last run in with Mary Ann and Bert, he wasn't sure it would be a good idea anyway.

Although Tom moved around a lot for work, mostly to the south of London, in Surrey and occasionally out as far as Kent, he regularly kept in touch with both Dick and Will, so they usually knew where he was. At the moment, he was working at a tannery near the River Mole in Leatherhead. One evening, at about 10 o' clock, just as Tom had got to bed after a long and tiring day's work, he heard a loud banging on the front door of the cheap, run down boarding house at which he was lodging. He heard his landlady grumbling loudly as she shuffled to the door in her carpet slippers.

"What do you want?" she demanded of the person at the door. "What time do you call this, to go disturbing decent folks what needs their rest?"

Tom heard the hubbub of conversation, but was drifting off to sleep so didn't catch much of it. Next minute, however, the banging came on his own bedroom door.

"Mr Finnimore, sir! I have an urgent message for you."

Tom leapt out of bed in a rush. Something terrible must have happened. His heart was pounding as he opened the door. A young man in messenger's uniform stood there.

"I've been sent by your brother Richard, sir," he told him. "He says please come at once. Your wife and son have arrived in Bermondsey and they need your help. Sorry to say, your wife is very ill."

Tom thanked the messenger, gave him a tip, then sat down heavily on the bed to try and take it all in. He was shaking. The landlady came in grumbling about all the disturbance, but she saw immediately that there was a genuine problem and her manner softened.

"I'll make you a nice brew, dearie," she offered. "That'll make you feel better."

Tom thought hurriedly what to do. He got himself dressed and packed his bag. After the promised brew he did feel a bit better, but knew that he had to leave immediately. He paid up for his room and sent a message to his workplace apologising for his sudden departure, then he left his lodgings and went out into the darkness, which promptly swallowed him up. In spite of it being late May, the rain was falling gently as he walked to the nearest station to catch the train up to London. His mind was reeling. What was Mary Ann doing up here again? What was the illness? Where was his daughter? He couldn't make any sense of it. The dark, wet night seemed to mirror his feelings of worry and confusion, and he was relieved when at last he was settled in a dry, warm railway carriage and was on the move.

He got to Dick and Eliza's in the early hours of the morning, just as Dick was getting up to go to work. The sun was up already, but Tom didn't feel any more cheerful. He was desperate to know what had happened.

They welcomed him warmly, then told him all they knew. Tom's son, John, had turned up unexpectedly at their house a couple of days ago, asking for help and very anxious to see Tom. The boy had taken some cheap lodgings in Marigold Street in Bermondsey, having accompanied his mother all the way from Bristol. Dick warned Tom that he would find Mary Ann much changed, in all ways.

After some breakfast, Eliza took Tom over to see them. Although Bermondsey's sanitation had much improved,

101

especially since Jacob's Island was built over in 1850, parts of Bermondsey were still poverty-stricken and the lodgings were as basic as they came, still having only outside cess pits, and the roughest and poorest of facilities. The street ran down towards the Thames, getting progressively more filthy and shambolic as it got nearer the water. Mary Ann and John were lodging about half way down the street in a small courtyard of ramshackle tenement flats, called Marigold Court. Tom and Eliza knocked and entered the front room, where they saw a young boy of about twelve years old, struggling to make a fire in the tiny hearth. He had light brown hair and was tall for his age, but looked weary and care-worn. Tom knew instantly that this was his son.

"John," he said and held out his arms towards him.

"Pa!" cried John and ran to him. They were both choked with emotion and no one said anything for a few minutes.

"Where's your mother?" asked Tom eventually. John led him upstairs to a dark and dingy bedroom, where Tom saw, with shock, his ex-wife. He barely recognised her. Her skin was of a yellow hue all over, including her eyes, which had always been such a beautiful, clear blue. Her legs and ankles were swollen up, even though she had lost a lot of weight from her body overall. The most horrible thing to Tom was to see the state of Mary Ann's hair. It had always been one of her greatest assets – lovely golden blonde curls which had framed her face – but now it was falling out and so thin you could see her scalp. He approached the bed warily.

"Mary Ann," he said. "It's me Tom, I've come as you asked."

She lifted her head off the pillow, gazing uncertainly at him.

"Who are you?" she asked. "I don't know you."

Tom went closer. "It's me, Mary Ann. Tom, your husband."

She seemed to remember him then, and reached out to him. He took her hands gently, noticing as he did, how curved her fingers were and how she grasped desperately at him.

"It's okay," he reassured her. "I'm here now."

"I wanted you so much, Tom," she managed. "I'm so sorry; you didn't deserve what I did to you."

"It's okay," he repeated. "We both made mistakes. Let's forget the past and just get you well again."

He tried to get her to tell him what had been happening to get her like this, but her memory was poor and she kept getting confused, so he left her to sleep. From what Tom gathered from his son later, Mary Ann had spent many years with Bert, gradually drinking more and going downhill in fortunes. After Bert lost his job in Alphington due to a particularly nasty argument with the boss, they moved away from Devon up to Bristol. At this stage Mary Ann had promised the children she would make a new start and she had really tried, but Bert's behaviour became erratic and even violent at times. Hannah refused to have him in the house, which unfortunately put a distance between herself and Mary Ann at a time when Mary Ann needed her most. John also told Tom that his sister, Molly, had become frightened by Bert's attitude towards her as she got older. He was increasingly leering and suggestive as she grew into an attractive young girl. This made Tom feel very angry, but luckily Molly had been sensible enough to spend more time with her Aunt whenever possible, and eventually Hannah offered to let her stay with her permanently. John was also offered a place to stay at his Aunt's but felt unable to leave Mary Ann. He was only ten years old then, but he understood that she was vulnerable and needed him. Not that Mary Ann seemed to appreciate either of the children; she had lost interest in them, the drink had deadened her feelings and she couldn't connect with them. She was drunk most of the time, in those days, and her health was beginning to suffer. She barely noticed on the occasions when Bert gave her a black eye. Things came to a head earlier that year, when Bert got into one drunken fight too many and was stabbed to death by an equally drunken combatant. It was at this stage that Mary Ann finally tried to obliterate herself with alcohol. The doctor was called and pronounced her riddled with liver disease, saying that if she didn't stop drinking she would die, and that the prognosis wasn't good either way. John appealed to his Aunt for help, but she said unless Mary Ann gave up the liquor she would not have her in the house, as she didn't want her anywhere near her children.

Now, a few months later, Mary Ann had suddenly realised she was dying, and although mentally very confused, knew she wanted to make peace with Tom. She insisted on travelling to London and going to Bermondsey to look for him. Her mind was totally fixed on this and she would not listen to anyone who tried to reason with her. It was young John who had to get them both safely there, obtain lodgings and then find Dick and Eliza. Mary Ann had some periods of lucidity, but was difficult and moody. When he finally got her to Marigold Court, she collapsed into bed and was not able to go any further.

After Mary Ann had gone back to sleep, Tom set about organising some things. The doctor was called and supplies of food, warm bedding and fuel for the fire were laid in. Tom spent a long time talking to his son about what had happened to Mary Ann, and he also took the opportunity to explain to him about their separation and why, as a father, he hadn't been there for him. John understood. He knew the truth in spite of his youthfulness. Eliza bustled around, making broth and cleaning up. Tom was grateful to her. She was a kind and motherly soul, and Tom thought again that it was sad that she'd had no children of her own.

The doctor, when he called, unfortunately gave them little hope. He prescribed some medicines to help alleviate the symptoms, but could not do more. Tom moved in with Mary Ann and John, although he slept downstairs. He worked together with John, and with help from Eliza, to make Mary Ann's last few weeks as comfortable as possible. He arranged to do a few hours of work at Jim's tannery here and there to keep some money coming in, but he was never away from home for very long. Jim was very understanding as he knew Tom so well.

Tom often sat with Mary Ann, trying to get her to eat or take medicine, but it was very difficult. Sometimes, she threw the bowls of food across the room. A lot of the time, she didn't even recognise him, and at other times she screamed at him in rage because he wouldn't get her a drink. She also had hallucinations which terrified her, leaving her trembling and crying with fear. She was wasting away in front of his eyes and he couldn't do anything to stop it, which made him feel absolutely helpless. Occasional, more lucid periods occurred when she would remember their old life in Clapham and reminisce about happier days. Tom knew this was not a very accurate picture of their life together, but he didn't attempt to destroy her illusions.

Once she asked him, "Why did I leave you, Tom? You were so good to me."

"It was just one of those things," he replied. "No one was to blame."

Then she started to cry. "I'm sorry!" she said. "I love you, Tom."

He comforted her until she slept again, but the next time she awoke, she had forgotten it all and her mood had changed.

In these weeks, Tom also got to know his son for the first time. He greatly admired the boy's resilience and his devotion to his mother. He had experienced things that no child should have to bear, and had come through it all bravely. John's eyes were open to his mother's faults, even though he still loved her dearly, and he had formed an important new relationship with his father. At last the pressure was off the young lad, and although he was sad to see his mother so ill, her care was no longer his sole responsibility. He was able to relax more and even smiled occasionally. Tom was also pleased to see John getting on well with Eliza. Her maternal nature was exactly what the boy needed at that moment. The three of them took turns to help care for Mary Ann, with Tom doing the 'lion's share', as he felt it was his duty.

After a few weeks, there was a sudden change for the worse. Mary Ann developed a high fever, alternately burning up or shivering. She also started vomiting blood and the Doctor advised them this was due to internal bleeding, and that unfortunately the end was near. Tom and John sat by her constantly; talking to her, soothing her, trying to cheer her. That afternoon, Mary Ann regained consciousness and, for once, was clear headed.

"Tom," she whispered. "I need to talk to you."

John understood and left the room.

"Try not to talk too much," said Tom. "You'll tire yourself."

"No, Tom, I must," she replied. "I don't have long left. I never meant to hurt you. I really did love you, but I wanted so much more. It was stupid, I know, now I've ended up with nothing. Bert was a bully and a brute. I wish I'd stayed with you. Do you still love me?" she asked.

It was an awkward question to answer. Tom had gone past all that and couldn't go back, but he wanted Mary Ann to be happy in her last hours. In spite of his passion for honesty, he managed to say, "Of course, Mary Ann. I've always loved you."

She smiled then, showing her bleeding gums and mouth. "Please, Tom, look after the children for me. I know they must hate me but I want them to be happy. Please tell them I'm sorry I let them down."

"Of course I'll look after them," he promised and he meant it. "Now please rest."

Mary Ann drifted off into unconsciousness again and Tom called John back in. There were tears in the lad's eyes. Eliza arrived, and after giving John a big hug, she made them all warm drinks. They all knew it wouldn't be long now. The watching and waiting was dreadful. At about 3 o' clock in the morning, as they dozed intermittently by her bedside, she sat up and cried out in distress, choking and vomiting blood again. They tried to ease her pain and discomfort, but a few minutes later she collapsed back onto the bed, never to stir again. Mary Ann had passed away at last.

Shortly after the simple funeral, Tom and his son John travelled to Bristol to see his daughter and Mary Ann's sister. John knew the address and so was able to direct him. Tom had already cabled Hannah the sad news of Mary Ann's passing and said they would be visiting.

The father and son had been getting on really well in the last few weeks, but Tom knew he couldn't offer the lad a proper home as he was always out working. Dick and Eliza had offered to look after him if he wanted to stay and John had accepted eagerly. He was very fond of his Aunty 'Liza and the couple were only too happy to have a child around at last. However, Tom felt John should talk to Molly and Hannah about it all before making a final commitment.

Tom felt nervous of meeting them both. He tried to imagine what Molly would look like now, but he could only picture her as a young child. They arrived at a middle class terraced house in the Southville area of Bristol. Hannah greeted them politely and introduced them to her family. He looked around, and suddenly saw a beautiful young girl of about 14 years old, who, he felt sure, must be his daughter. He was shocked by how much she reminded him of his ex-wife. She had light golden brown ringlets and blue eyes just like Mary Ann, but was wearing a black armband. To his surprise, she hung back from the rest of the family as if reluctant to say hello.

"Molly?" he asked nervously.

"Father," she said and took a step forward, but she only shook his hand.

The meeting was stiff and formal and Tom felt rather awkward. He told Molly and Hannah a little about Mary Ann's death, but refrained from telling the more unpleasant details. There were some things, he thought, better left unsaid. Then he asked Molly how she was and what her plans were for the future. Molly was clear on one thing – she wanted to stay with her Aunt Hannah in Bristol. Hannah was a rather prim and proper sort of lady, with ideas slightly above her station, although it was true that her husband earned a reasonable income and that the family was financially secure. Her plans for Molly, she told Tom, were to get her into service in a rich household with a good reputation, and then hopefully to get her married off.

"Is that what *you* want to do?" Tom asked Molly.

"Whatever Aunt Hannah says is fine with me. She helped me when I needed someone," she replied stiffly.

"I'm sorry I couldn't be there," said Tom. "But it wasn't my fault." He could see that she didn't believe him.

"Why did you abandon us, Father?" she asked suddenly. "We needed you!"

"It wasn't like that!" he protested. "I didn't know where you were. I promised your mother I'd look after you now and I will."

"I think it's too late for that, Father," she replied coldly. "You didn't protect me from Bert, so why should you bother now?"

There was an embarrassing silence. Tom didn't know what to say. He felt guilty, but wasn't quite sure why.

"What about you, John?" asked Hannah, after a pause, turning towards him. "Do you want to come here as well? You'd be welcome."

John went red. "Not to be rude," he answered, "but I want to stay with Aunty 'Liza and Uncle Dick in London. I'm sorry but I don't really like it here."

So it was decided, and although the two children shed a few tears as they parted again, Tom promised to make sure everyone kept in touch. They'd already spent some time apart in any case, and seemed to be headed in quite different directions.

Tom tried to embrace Molly as he left but she just turned away.

"Goodbye, Father," was all she said.

Chapter 20
Godalming, Surrey, 1859

The tall, dark haired woman at the door eyed Tom suspiciously. She was dressed plainly, her long hair tied back in a bun.

"I need someone for several months," she said.

"I don't usually stay for that long," he replied hesitantly, "but maybe I could this time."

He had been told by the last yard he had been at in Shalford that they needed someone here urgently, and that the owner, a widow called Phyllis Stedman, would pay well to a skilled tanner.

"What are you running away from then?" she asked directly.

Her dark eyes were keenly intelligent but good-humoured.

Tom laughed nervously. "Well," he said. "I, 'er, well, I mean…"

"Oh don't worry!" said the woman. "It's none of my business! It doesn't worry me as long as you won't disappear off without warning. I need the help while my chief tanner's off with a broken leg. Are you any good? I've got to have a yard manager who knows all the stages of the process, to oversee everything and keep the rest of them working. Can you do it or can't you?"

She was blunt but not rude. Tom liked her directness and decided to give it a try.

"I can, ma'am," replied Tom confidently and proceeded to tell her his experience.

"Well," she agreed when he paused. "It seems you certainly have all the skills I need. But don't think you can put one over on me just because I'm a woman! I may have been a widow for a while now but I know what I'm doing. My husband was a skilled tanner and employed many workers. I know all about the process and I will be able to tell if you're not doing what you should."

"You don't need to worry about me, ma'am," Tom reassured her. "I always work hard and do a good job. No one has ever complained about me. Here are my references if you want them."

"I don't need them," the woman replied. "I make up my own mind about people. But firstly – don't call me ma'am anymore. It makes me sound like the Queen! Just call me Phyllis, or Mrs Stedman if you really want to, but I'd rather you didn't. You'll find my eldest son William is one of your workers as well. He's only seventeen and still learning, but don't make any concessions for him. He needs to work just as hard as the rest of them. I'd also like regular reports from you on how everything's going."

She then showed Tom the small cottage on site that he would be able to live in whilst he was there. It was shared with another labourer, and although basic, it was clean and comfortable. There wasn't much room, but Tom had very few possessions anyway. His room had a single bed, a table with a lamp on it and a cupboard for his things. There was a small kitchen, a parlour and washing facilities in the cottage as well, so it was quite cosy.

"Evening meals are served up at the main house at 7 pm," explained Phyllis and she told him the daily routine. "Feel free to come and go at any time. We have a pretty open house here." She smiled suddenly and her face lit up. "I hope you'll be happy here," she said.

"I'm sure I will," he replied, and this time he meant it. There was something open, honest and direct in her that he liked. It was a refreshing change.

Much to his surprise, Tom enjoyed being in charge of the tanning yard. He had never overseen the whole process before but he had years of experience to call on, and so he found it easy to adapt to this new role. For the first few days, he watched carefully how they all worked together. He didn't want to go barging in, changing things immediately, as he was the 'new boy'. However, after this brief period, he began to suggest small improvements to their ways of working and soon had them collaborating very efficiently as a team. They liked him and respected him, and he began to settle in well. In the evenings he joined the rest of the 'live-in' workers over at the big house for supper. Some of them were curious about him and asked him

110

questions. He was a bit reticent with his answers at first, until Phyllis got involved and then he felt he had to reply.

"Where do you come from?" they wanted to know.

"Here and there," he said. "I've been all over the place."

"But where's home?" asked Phyllis.

"Oh I'm not sure about that," replied Tom laughing. "But my family come from Devon, near Exeter."

"Why didn't you stay down there?" she persisted.

"Well," he said awkwardly. "I was looking for more work so I came to Bermondsey Leather Market and then moved further out."

He could feel himself going red with embarrassment. He didn't know them well enough to share his story with them. Luckily Phyllis let it drop and the talk returned to more general matters.

A couple of weeks went by, and Tom was becoming concerned about one of the workers – unfortunately it was Phyllis's son William. He seemed moody and depressed. His work was lacklustre and shoddy at times. Tom decided to have a word with him, and at the end of the working day, called him over to talk to.

"Come and sit down," said Tom kindly. "Let's have a chat."

William scowled but obeyed.

"I get the feeling you're not very happy doing this," Tom started.

"I hate it!" William burst out then went red. "Sorry, but it's a dreadful job. The smell! It's disgusting."

"Why are you doing it then?" asked Tom.

"Because Dad died and Mum expected me to fill in for him and take over the business one day. I can't let her down, but I hate it!"

"What do you really want to do?" questioned Tom.

"I'd love to be a farmer," William replied enthusiastically. "I'd be happy working in the fields with animals and crops. I worked at the farm next door when I was younger and I learnt so much."

Tom remembered his initial feelings about tanning and felt sorry for the lad. It was this that had caused all his problems in the first place.

"Can't you tell your mother?" Tom asked the boy, but William just shook his head sadly. "Look William," he said, "maybe I could talk to your mother and explain how you feel about it."

"Oh, please!" cried William. "Would you?"

"Yes," said Tom. "But in the meantime you've got to sharpen up your work. I know you hate it and I can understand that. I felt that way myself at first."

"Really?" asked William, astonished.

"Yes, really," asserted Tom. "But it passed eventually and it may do for you. You *do* get used to it in the end. However, I'm happy to talk to your mother, as long as you make more of an effort. You need to pull your weight and prove yourself. You're letting the rest of your workmates down."

"I will try harder," said William. "Thank you."

Tom wasn't sure what he was going to say to Phyllis about this, but he had promised to try and he wasn't going to let the boy down. So one evening, after the meal, he lingered after the rest of the labourers went out. As it happened, she seemed keen to talk to him.

"Tom," she said smiling, "how's it going? I keep hearing good things about you. The men seem happy and the work's going well. Sit down. Tell me all about it."

Tom started by giving her a general report on the work and then turned to the subject he wanted to talk about really – William. He was nervous, but hoped that a direct and honest approach would go down well with her and that she wouldn't get angry or be offended.

"Well, this is a bit awkward," he began. "I wanted to talk to you about William."

"Why, what's he done now?" she asked, sighing heavily. "He's always causing trouble, that boy. I don't know why."

"Well, I do know a bit about it," Tom explained. "William's a good lad and tries his best, but he absolutely hates the work. He's only doing it to please you. I understand how he feels because I went through it myself and it caused me no end of trouble."

Phyllis looked surprised. "What do you mean, he hates it? He never said anything."

"He feels he has to do it because you want him to take his father's place," Tom told her. "He really wants to be a farmer."

Phyllis was silent, taking it all in.

"I'm sorry," said Tom. "I know it's none of my business really, but he wasn't working very well so I had to have a word with him and then he told me. I *have* told him he needs to shape up, but I *did* say I'd talk to you about it as well."

There was a pause and Tom was afraid he had annoyed her, but when she spoke her voice was choked with emotion.

"So what you're saying is that I've forced him into doing something he hates," she said.

"I wouldn't have put it quite like that," Tom said awkwardly. "But basically, yes, I suppose so. Sorry!"

"Thank you for being so honest with me," she said. "I appreciate it and will certainly do something about it. But tell me more about yourself – what trouble did it cause *you*?"

"I'm not sure you really want to hear my story," he mumbled. "It's a bit embarrassing really."

"You keep yourself to yourself a lot, don't you?" she observed. "But I won't be shocked by anything you tell me, honestly. I'm interested in you and I want to know more. Why don't I get you a beer and then we can talk?"

So they sat by the fire in the cosy parlour, almost as friends, just talking. It was warm and comfortable in the firelight, and easy to relax. Tom was ashamed of his past and hesitated to start with, but then he found himself telling her how much he had hated tanning, especially when his girlfriend had rejected him.

"That was a mean thing to do," said Phyllis. "She obviously didn't really care about you."

"Well," said Tom, "it gets worse! I got very drunk and did something stupid and I – well I – oh I can't tell you. I'm too ashamed!"

He hung his head in shame, but Phyllis patted his arm in a kindly manner.

"Come off it, Tom. Whatever it is, it doesn't matter."

"But you'll think badly of me," he said. "And maybe send me away."

"What are you?" she exclaimed, slightly alarmed. "An axe murderer?"

This made him laugh and he felt more able to tell her.

113

"No, not as bad as that!" he cried. "I stole six chickens and went to prison for it."

Phyllis laughed loudly. "Is that all?" she cried. "Tell me all about it."

So Tom told her the whole sorry story of how he ended up in the hulks, followed by Millbank prison. He also told her, more proudly, of how he was eventually pardoned. Phyllis followed it all closely, asking him questions about how he felt and what he did to survive. Tom realised he had never had the chance to tell anyone this before (Mary Ann had never wanted to discuss it). It felt good to let it all out at last.

"But what about you?" he said at last. "I don't know anything about you. That's not fair."

"There's not much to tell," answered Phyllis. "I've been widowed for just over a year now. George was a good man, always hard-working and reliable, although so busy there were times when I rarely saw him. He died of cancer. It wasn't an easy death, unfortunately."

They talked late into the evening, until Tom suddenly remembered he had to work the next day.

He got up and made to leave, saying, "Thank you for listening to me. It's made me feel a lot better."

"I've a feeling there's even more for you to tell," said Phyllis. "Why not stay and chat another evening? I'm glad of the company. There's only William and Jack otherwise, and it's not the same as talking to another adult." (Jack was Phyllis's youngest son who was only 10 years old and was just about to finish school)

"I'd love to," Tom told her. "It's good to have a friend."

Their friendship progressed steadily with regular chats about all kinds of things. Tom ended up telling her about his difficulty in adapting to life after prison, and he admitted his subsequent fear of crowds and his panic attacks. Unlike Mary Ann, Phyllis understood and didn't make fun of him. They talked about the Coronation and Tom told Phyllis what had happened and how good Lizzie had been to him. Phyllis and her husband, George, had also been up for the Coronation and they reminisced about what they had seen. He also talked about his family in Devon and his love for the area. They exchanged views on everything from politics to favourite foods.

Phyllis was easy to talk to and a good listener. She took it all in and then asked intelligent questions. In return, she told him all about trying to bring up four children since George had died and about trying to keep the yard going. She expressed her worries about her fifteen year old daughter (also called Phyllis, but known as Fliss because she could never say the name 'Phyllis' when she was a young child), who was working as a kitchen maid for the local curate. She was open about her feelings of guilt in sending Fliss and William out to work at so young an age. They'd both been working a few years now already.

"At least Caroline, my oldest, is married and settled now," she said. "That's a weight off my mind."

Tom agreed, but thought about his own children and wondered if he should mention them, but couldn't quite bring himself to.

One evening, Phyllis was talking intimately about her relationship with George.

"He was quite a bit older than me," she told him. "More of a father-figure, I suppose. I lost my own father when I was quite young and I needed someone to look up to. However, as we got older, the age gap began to be a problem for us. He didn't want to travel or experience new things. I wanted to go the Great Exhibition, but we didn't because he was so busy working." (Tom had already told her how he had taken Lizzie there and what a great time they'd had). "We hadn't been 'close' in years, if you know what I mean. He said he had four children already and didn't see the point." She sighed.

The only thing Tom hadn't talked about so far was his marriage and his children. He was a bit shocked, therefore, when the thorny subject suddenly reared its head.

"What about you, Tom?" she asked. "Have you ever married?"

It was almost too much for him and his instinct was to leave. He stood up, but something made him stay. Phyllis saw the distress on his face and knew something was wrong.

"I'm sorry!" she said. "I shouldn't have asked."

Tom swallowed hard. "No, it's okay," he told her. "I need to tell someone, but it's hard. I'm not sure I'm ready. Can we call it a night?"

"Of course," replied Phyllis and watched him go off to his cottage. She felt sad that she'd upset him. If only she hadn't been so curious, she thought to herself.

Tom spent a long and sleepless night. His mind was racing with memories of the past, turning things over and over, but his main concern, oddly enough, was for Phyllis. He hoped she wasn't angry at him and he knew he needed to talk it all out with her. He would hate to lose her friendship, which was so valuable to him. He eventually fell asleep just before dawn, only about an hour before he needed to rise for work. Later that morning, he saw Phyllis across the yard and hurried over to her. There were other workers around so his tone was formal.

"I need to talk to you about some issues this evening," he said. "Can I see you after supper, please?"

She nodded, but her face was anxious. "That's fine. I'll see you then," she replied.

Tom ate barely any supper that night and he was very quiet. One of the other workers asked him if he was feeling alright, as he was clearly not himself.

"I'm fine, thanks," he muttered, but he wasn't really.

He now had his emotions just about under control, but he was nervous of broaching this subject with anyone, let alone Phyllis. After the others had left, however, he followed Phyllis into the parlour, shutting the door firmly behind them.

"I need to talk to you," he began.

"Look Tom," she said. "You don't have to tell me anything. I'm so sorry I upset you."

He held up his hand to silence her. "No, listen," he said, gazing directly into her eyes. "I must tell this to someone and you are the only friend I have, apart from my family. Would you do me the honour of listening to it, please? I hope you won't judge me too harshly."

They settled comfortably in the armchairs and Tom started nervously.

"You once asked whether I was running away from something, and it's true, I was. I *have* been married, but my wife died last year. Our marriage didn't work out though and we'd been separated for years. I also have two children, who now live with their aunts and uncles."

He watched her face for any signs of disapproval but she smiled gently.

"Go on," she encouraged him.

So Tom told Phyllis the whole story, bit by bit, starting with meeting Mary Ann again in Devon, then her coming to London, their marriage, having children and getting into debt. Tom found himself getting quite emotional when he told her about their separation. From time to time, Phyllis expressed her views on Mary Ann's behaviour, which were not favourable. She shocked Tom by saying she thought Mary Ann was selfish and vain.

"Oh no, really!" he protested.

"Look Tom," she insisted. "She hurt you, spent all your money and stole your children. I'm sorry, but what is there to like about her?"

"Maybe, you're right," he admitted. "I've never thought of it that way before."

"I think you've blamed yourself far too much," said Phyllis. "But you didn't need to, believe me."

Tom then told Phyllis about his attempts at keeping in touch with his children, and then about Mary Ann's death. Phyllis sympathised, but again reassured Tom that none of it was his fault.

"You did everything you could," she said.

"My daughter hates me," sighed Tom. "She doesn't understand."

"She will one day," Phyllis told him, "and at least your son, John knows the truth. Why did you never talk about this before?"

"Well, my family know most of it I suppose, but they don't really know how I feel. You're the first person I've ever opened up to." He looked up at her. "You're so easy to talk to."

"I'm pleased that you trusted me," Phyllis responded, and held his hand briefly. "Come on, let's have a drink."

The mood was lightened and Tom felt much relieved. The burden was lifted at last.

After a period of many weeks, there wasn't much they didn't know about each other. They were the best of friends and Tom looked forward to seeing Phyllis in the evenings. In the meantime, she had acted on what Tom said about William. She spoke to her son directly and offered him the chance to go and learn farming, which he jumped at. Before he left, William found

Tom and thanked him profusely, but Tom waved it aside. He was just glad to see the lad happy. Of course, this left the yard short-handed, but the man who'd been off with the broken leg was due back fairly soon, so they should be okay.

Tom worried however, that this meant he wouldn't be needed any more and he suddenly realised that he didn't want to leave here. He was frightened at the thought that he might be replaced. About three months after he started, he came in on Monday morning to hear that Ed was returning the following week, and that Phyllis wanted to speak to him. His heart sank. Of course, he thought, he had only ever been a temporary hiring. Hadn't he told her himself that he couldn't stay long? Now he regretted that. How could he face moving on from here? It felt so right, almost like home.

Reluctantly, he went up to the big house to see Phyllis. He knew straight away that this was a formal meeting. Her usual warm, easygoing approach had been replaced by a stiff awkwardness.

"I need to talk to you, Tom," she began. "As I'm sure you've heard, Ed is due back next week."

Tom nodded silently.

"As I expect you remember, we both agreed at the start that your appointment was only temporary."

"I understand," Tom replied.

She raised her hand to silence him as she continued, "What I'm wondering now is whether you would consider staying on a more permanent basis. I know you said you don't usually stay anywhere very long, so I'm not sure what you would think about this, but I feel that you've done a very good job and you seem to have settled in well. I think we would all be lost without you." She moved closer, gazing at him. "In fact, I personally would be lost without you, Tom," she said quietly. "What do you say?"

Tom heaved a sigh of relief. "I thought you were going to get rid of me!" he exclaimed. "I know what I said, but this is different. I like it here and I'd love to stay."

"Really?" said Phyllis. "That's wonderful."

"The only thing is," said Tom, "that obviously I'll go back to just working as a tanner in the yard, because Ed will need to have his job back and take over again."

"Well," Phyllis told him, "not quite. I've spoken to Ed and he feels managing the whole yard would be too much for him now. I've offered him the foreman's job and he's accepted. He says he's happy to have a bit less responsibility. So would you carry on as yard manager, please? You've made lots of improvements and the men like you."

"Won't they all think I'm pushing Ed out and stealing his job, though?" asked Tom.

"No," she reassured him. "I'll explain it all to them. There won't be any resentment, I'm sure of it."

"Well in that case," replied Tom, "I'd be only too happy."

Chapter 21

Tom settled down happily and soon found a good workmate and friend in Ed. Ed Johnson was in his fifties with a large family, and had always lived locally. He was able to tell Tom a lot about the area and he always knew the local gossip. They got on well and often had a good laugh together.

The evening conversations with Phyllis continued and he felt comfortable there. On Sundays, he sometimes walked down by the River Wey in Godalming town, or by the Wey and Arun Canal. He was amused by the quirky little pepper-pot shaped town hall. They'd had nothing like that in Devon. Ed was right, he thought; it was a nice town, although at times he still hankered after the rolling Devon hills. Godalming was situated in a valley, with a large meadow known as the Lammas land, somewhat prone to flooding. The town was sited between, and on the sides of two hills, it was true, but was not quite the same as Tom had been used to when he grew up. It was more thickly wooded than Devon, but with less farmland.

Ever since Mary Ann had died Tom, had visited his son John every couple of weeks at the weekend, either seeing him at Dick and Eliza's or taking him out around London. Sometimes they went to a tea room, walked through the parks or down by the Thames. John was growing into a fine young man, mature and sensible. Tom was proud of him, but knew it was mostly due to the loving home provided for him by Dick and Eliza. They had all become very close and Eliza was like a mother to him. Tom wasn't jealous, in fact, he was pleased to see them all so happy. He enjoyed his son's company and was pleased to be able to advise him on matters of life. They had had very little contact with Molly, but they knew she was okay and that Hannah was busy trying to find her a respectable household to work in.

One Sunday, not long after his appointment as manager had been made permanent, Tom spent the whole time enthusiastically talking about his new life. Eliza teased him, saying he'd spent all afternoon talking about Phyllis.

"You want to watch it, Tom! Sounds like you're quite taken with this woman. You'll be walking out with her next."

"We're just friends," he claimed, but blushed in spite of himself.

The next time he was out with John on their own, he was surprised by the boy asking him whether he would ever get married again.

"No, I can't see that happening," answered Tom. "Once was enough."

"What about this woman at work?" John asked (He was perceptive enough to have heard what Eliza said and to have realised what it meant). "You won't replace Ma, will you?" he added anxiously.

"Of course not," replied Tom. "Don't worry, Phyllis is just a friend," he reassured him. "No one could replace your mother."

Tom had arrived in Godalming in the summer of 1859, but now it was late autumn and the days were getting shorter and colder. It was dark in the morning when they started work, and dark when they finished. Increasingly often, they had to break the ice on the soaking vats before they could use them. The newly developing leather didn't respond well to the cold, either, so they worked hard to keep it as warm and pliable as possible. Phyllis laid in extra supplies of fuel for fires and stoves to help. She also worked tirelessly to provide them all with hot drinks and meals.

Usually, Tom went to church every Sunday in Godalming town. This was mostly because all the men from the yard went there, including Ed and his family, and it was always good to get together socially. It also meant that afterwards Tom could either walk around the town or catch the train to London to see his family. The yard itself was actually in Farncombe, an area of Godalming that was, at that stage, still a village in its own right. Tom liked this because it reminded him of Alphington. It had an alehouse, several small businesses and a church of its own. One Sunday in particular, Tom decided to go to St John's Church in Farncombe instead. He had slipped on a patch of ice in the yard that morning and bruised his knee. It wasn't serious, but it hurt enough to make him reluctant to walk too far. He'd been back to

London the weekend before, so he figured he would just have a restful day and let it heal. At the church he was a bit embarrassed to see Phyllis with her whole family. He knew both her sons well, of course, but had not met either of her daughters before. He noticed how fine she looked in her Sunday best, and suddenly realised that she was, in fact, quite a handsome woman. Phyllis saw him and smiled from a distance during the service. Afterwards, she made a point of coming over to see him.

"You're limping, Tom!" she exclaimed with concern. "What's wrong?"

He explained that it was nothing serious and he saw her breathe a sigh of relief. Then she introduced him to Caroline, James (Caroline's husband) and her younger daughter, Fliss. They said their 'hello's' politely. The older boy, William, who was now farming, was keen to see Tom again and tell him all about his work.

"If you're not doing anything this afternoon, why not join us for tea?" said Phyllis. "I can see William here is dying to tell you all about his new job."

"That would be nice," replied Tom and accompanied them to a small tea room in Farncombe village where they all had tea and cakes.

William chattered away enthusiastically to Tom, telling him all about what he'd been doing at work, and Tom was pleased to hear how happy he was. The younger son, Jack, had recently been showing an interest in the tanning yard, and although only ten years old and a bit too young to work, Tom promised to show him around and explain the process to him. The daughters were quiet at first, listening to him talking to the boys, but then Caroline suddenly asked Tom about himself.

"Do you have any children?" she said.

"Yes, a girl and a boy," he answered.

"Don't they live with you?" she asked, surprised.

"No, they are living with their Aunts and Uncles. I am a widower," he replied.

"Don't you think they should be living with their father?" she pursued.

"Caroline, really!" protested her mother.

"It's okay," said Tom. "The trouble is, you see, I am always working so I don't have enough time to look after them properly."

"How old are they?" asked Fliss.

"Thirteen and fifteen now," replied Tom. "My daughter is about the same age as you, actually."

"At least I have my mother," she remarked. "And I can remember my dear father clearly. He was wonderful. No one can ever replace him!"

This struck Tom as a slightly odd thing for her to say, but all he said was, "Of course not. No one can replace your parents. I know I still miss mine."

He smiled at her, but she looked at him suspiciously. He could see that she had some hidden agenda that he couldn't quite place. The older daughter, Caroline, was pregnant with her first child, the baby being due in the New Year, so she spent time talking about their plans. He could sense she didn't approve of him for some reason. She also mentioned her father and, sighing, wished he could have been around to see her forthcoming baby.

"It's so important for a child to have their family," she said pointedly, looking at Tom whilst she spoke.

The tea having been drunk, Tom politely made his excuses and left. He was feeling uncomfortable, although he couldn't quite put his finger on the reason why. He dismissed it from his mind therefore, and went for a gentle stroll through the village before heading home. The following week, Phyllis apologised for her two daughters' behaviour, but Tom denied there was any problem with it.

"They were just curious," he said. "That's all."

"Well, I've told them not to be so rude in future," Phyllis replied.

Although Tom returned to Godalming church as normal, the following week he did pay one more visit to Farncombe again in the time leading up to Christmas. It was the first Sunday of Advent and the church was lit with candles. Tom loved this time of year. He wasn't quite sure why he chose to go there that week, but if he was honest with himself, it was to see Phyllis and her family again. After the service, he stopped to say hello to them all again and to wish them a happy Christmas time. The two girls were rather subdued this time, but their mother, Phyllis, was the same as ever.

"What are you doing at Christmas, Tom?" she asked.

"I'll be going back to see my family in London," he told her.

She looked a little disappointed. "I was hoping maybe you could spend a little time with us," she said. "What about New Year?"

"Well, I will be around at that time," said Tom.

"Why not come to lunch that day?" invited Phyllis. "We're quite traditional and still give our gifts then. It'll be a real family occasion."

"Oh yes, please do!" cried William and Jack together. "It'd be great to have you there."

"Why not bring your son as well?" suggested Phyllis. "I'd like to meet him."

"That'd be great, I'd love to," replied Tom warmly and he left them, feeling very happy indeed. However, after he departed, the two daughters turned on her.

"Why did you do that, Mother?" they demanded. "He's not our family. We don't want him there!"

"He's a very dear friend of mine," said Phyllis firmly. "And it's my house, so I'll invite who I like. If you don't like it, don't come!"

"I think you're sweet on him, Mother!" retorted Caroline. "And I don't like it. It's not right. It's an insult to Father's memory. He's only been dead a year!"

Young Fliss agreed, her eyes filling with tears as she spoke. "He's not our father and we don't want a replacement."

"Don't be silly!" exclaimed Phyllis, angry now. "He's a loyal employee and a good friend. That's all!" Even as she said this, however, she knew she wasn't really being honest with them or herself.

When Tom spoke to his son John about coming down to Godalming for the New Year, he was dismayed by his reaction.

"I don't want to," he said sulkily. "That woman will be there. She's not my mother."

"Of course she isn't," Tom replied. "Just come and meet her. She's a great friend."

But nothing he could say would change the lad's mind, so they just agreed to spend Christmas Day together and nothing more. Tom did his best to smooth things over with John, but was disappointed, nonetheless. He made a feeble excuse to Phyllis for the boy's absence and she made a similar one for her daughters, who had also refused to be there. Her two sons were going to be there however, and Tom was looking forward to it. Now that Christmas was really taking off as an occasion (due to Queen Victoria's influence) there were feasts and gifts, and most strangely of all, a decorated tree in the home! Tom found it very amusing that people would bring in a tree from outside and even hang ornaments on it, when normally they wouldn't even consider it, except for firewood! It seemed absurd. But as he saw the festivities beginning over in the big house he began to feel quite excited by it all in spite of himself. Christmas Day was spent in Bermondsey and Tom took small gifts for everyone, which he hung on their own small tree. He'd also sent gifts to Bristol for Molly, Hannah and the family. On the day, a feast of roast beef was consumed and they played games and sang songs together as a family. Tom and his son, John, were back on good terms again and all was well.

On Boxing Day, Tom was back in the yard again, but there wasn't much going on. At lunchtime, Phyllis came out to the workers with presents for them all, and she also told them to go home early. She gave out boxes of fruit, sweets, nuts and bottles of ale, along with gifts of meat for the families. Tom saw what a good employer she was to her workers and admired her for it. He thanked her for his box and turned to go back to his cottage, but she touched his arm gently.

"Come and join me at the house for a drink, Tom."

It was a warm and cosy afternoon sat by the fire; talking, drinking, eating. Later that day, some carol singers came around and Phyllis invited them in for hot punch and sweet Christmas pies. Tom thought he had never had such a good time at Christmas before.

At New Year, he gave Phyllis and the two boys' small gifts of hand carved trinket boxes made from leather. He had spent a lot of time on these himself, and was quite proud of his efforts. Phyllis was delighted with hers. She gave Tom a large wooden box to keep some of his possessions in and he was truly happy. It was a wonderful meal and a very happy day; a great way to start 1860. He remembered New Year's Day in 1834, when he was sentenced for his crime, and marvelled at how things could change.

Chapter 22

It was a cold frosty morning about half way through January when Phyllis came across the yard and called everyone together.

"As you know," she said, "my eldest daughter Caroline is due to give birth to her first baby very soon, so I will be going to stay with her for a while to help out. I am taking my son Jack with me and I have engaged a woman from the village to cook the evening meals and do the cleaning whilst I am away. I don't expect it will be for more than a couple of weeks. Tom will be in charge of the yard, so if there's any problems talk to him. I'm sure you'll all do fine without me, anyway. We shall be leaving tomorrow."

This event had been on the cards for quite a while, so no one was surprised by the announcement. Tom, however, felt dismayed at the prospect of not having her around for a while. The men went back to work and Phyllis turned to Tom.

"I'm sure I can rely on you to look after everything for me," she said smiling. "You're a good manager. I couldn't have made a better choice."

"I hope everything goes well," Tom replied. "Wish Caroline all the best for me." He paused. "I'll miss you," he added.

"It won't be for long," Phyllis reassured him and then she went back to the house to finish getting ready.

The day developed into a bright, sunny but cold one which should have lifted his spirits, but somehow didn't. Tom felt gloomy already.

The first week went by and Tom didn't feel too bad, although he missed their chats in the evenings. During the second week, however, he really began to feel lost and miserable. Every evening seemed so long and empty. Still, he consoled himself, she should be back soon. They heard, via Bess the cleaning woman, that Caroline had had her baby (a girl) that week, but that it hadn't been an easy birth. Apparently she was still very weak. Tom still hoped that Phyllis would be home soon, but they entered the third week and there was no sign of her. Now he was beginning to feel desperate, and towards the end of the week, he tried to get more information out of Bess.

"Well dearie," she said. "Caroline's a lot better now, so maybe your Mistress will be back next week."

All had gone well in the yard, but Tom was sad and lonely.

Ed noticed and said, "Hey, what's up mate? You look like you lost a shilling!"

"I'm fine," muttered Tom.

"You don't look it!" exclaimed Ed. "How about coming over to lunch with the family on Sunday? Cheer you up a bit."

Tom agreed readily and enjoyed the outing, but he saw Ed with his wife and family and realised what he was missing. He came home that afternoon to his lonely cottage, missing Phyllis more than ever. Monday morning of the fourth week dawned and Tom felt he couldn't cope any more without her. He knew now that he needed her, and more than that, he loved her. Why he hadn't realised it before, he didn't know. He would have to tell her. His nights that week were long and sleepless while he rehearsed in his mind, over and over, what to say to her and how she might react. He knew they were close and that she was fond of him, but what would happen if he told her what he really felt?

On the Thursday morning that week, Tom saw a horse and cart pull up at the house, and Phyllis and her son John got off with their bags. Tom was delighted. He couldn't wait to see her again. He bustled around the yard for a while, organising things, then suddenly announced to the men that he was going up to the house to see the mistress and give his report on the last few weeks. Ed smiled. He had a feeling he knew what kind of report Tom would be making! Tom rushed over, his heart pounding in his chest. Phyllis saw him coming and opened the door, smiling. As she shut the door behind him all the words came tumbling out, completely unlike the careful speeches he'd rehearsed to himself.

"Dearest Phyllis. I missed you so much!"

Without stopping to think, he took her in his arms and kissed her, and to his joy, she responded with equal enthusiasm.

But after a minute, she pulled gently away, saying, "Really Tom, we mustn't. This isn't right."

"I love you, Phyllis!" he cried. "How can it not be right? I realised while you were away that I can't live without you."

"Oh, Tom," she murmured, tears in her eyes. "You know I'm very fond of you, but we can't do this! My daughters aren't happy about it. They think I'm being disloyal to their father just by being friends. It's too soon after his death. I can't upset them. I'm sorry."

"My son feels the same," protested Tom. "But it's not their lives, it's ours! We deserve to be happy. Besides, you said yourself, you weren't close to George in later years."

"I know," she agreed. "But the other thing is that I'm your employer and the men in the yard might not like it. They'll see it as favouritism. We all have to work together. It could be very awkward."

Tom stared at her, disappointed. He didn't know what to say.

"Please understand, Tom," Phyllis said. "Let's just stay friends like we were."

"I'm not sure I can," he replied. "I'll try, but I can't promise anything. Things have changed."

He turned and walked out of the house and back to the yard. One of the workers asked him a question about some supplies, but he just snapped at him. He knew he shouldn't have, but he felt so wretched he wanted to die. He apologised later because he knew it wasn't the man's fault. That evening, he didn't go over to the house for supper. He just had bread and cheese in his cottage on his own. When he was quite alone in his bed he tossed and turned, spending yet another sleepless night trying to understand everything. He didn't see how he could just be friends with her any more. Hadn't she kissed him back with all her heart? He felt sure she loved him, really. Towards the early hours of the morning, he more or less came to terms with her reasons and hoped that things might change in the future. He would, he decided, try and stay friends, to give things a chance. Maybe the passing of time would help. The following couple of evenings he appeared for supper as normal, and tried to be polite and sociable.

Even so, on Friday evening, when Phyllis asked him to stay for a while, he replied, "I'm sorry. I've got things to do," and he went back to his cottage. He couldn't face being intimate with her again quite yet.

On Saturday evening, Tom was fast asleep in bed when he heard a banging on the door. It was just before eleven o'clock and he wondered who it could possibly be. A messenger stood there, asking for him and Tom's heart sank.

"I have a message for you, sir," he announced and read: 'Your daughter Molly needs you urgently. Please come to Bristol at once. Regards Hannah.'

His pulse pounded. Something dreadful must have happened. Perhaps she was ill, or had had an accident. He questioned the messenger but he knew nothing more. Tom knew there was a late train to London, which he could catch if he left immediately. He dressed, threw some things hurriedly in a bag then banged on his fellow lodger's door.

"I have to go away to see my daughter for a few days. I don't know when I'll be back. Let Phyllis know and ask Ed to cover for me."

"What?" said Jake sleepily. "You're going away?"

"Yes," said Tom. "Tell them at the house."

Jake wasn't really taking anything in; he'd been out drinking and was half asleep already. He muttered that he'd let them know, then Tom knew he'd have to go or he'd miss the train. If he caught that one he could catch one for Bristol tomorrow morning and get there on Sunday. Tom knew he mustn't let Molly down this time. He briefly considered going up to the house or around to Ed's to tell them, but it was very late. They'd all be asleep and besides, he would probably miss the train. He couldn't leave a note either as he still hadn't learnt to write, so he had to pray Jake would give them the right message. He went out into the freezing cold February night, hoping for the best.

Tom got to Bristol on Sunday afternoon after a terrible day spent frantically worrying about Molly. When he knocked on the door of Hannah's house he was somewhat surprised, therefore, to find his daughter opening it. She looked perfectly well and Tom was amazed.

"Molly!" he exclaimed. "I thought you were ill. I was told to come here urgently."

"Father!" said Molly joyfully. "I'm glad you've come. I need you to act as a referee for me tomorrow at a job interview. It's a very respectable house and they'll only consider me if I bring a parent along. Aunt Hannah said she'd ask you. I'm so pleased you're here. I really didn't think you would. Thank you!"

Tom sighed. There was a mixture of emotions inside him – relief that Molly was okay and that she was pleased to see him, anger at Hannah's deception and worry about his job and Phyllis. Nevertheless, he made the best of it by doing everything Molly wanted. He was pleased that she was accepting him again and he felt that maybe, by doing this for her, their relationship could be restored. When he got Hannah alone, however, he accused her of deceiving him. She just claimed to have accidentally missed telling him all the truth due to the lack of time.

"Would you have come anyway," she asked, "if you had known the reason?"

"Yes, of course," replied Tom. "But I would have been able to make better arrangements at work."

He worried now what people might be thinking of him back in Farncombe, especially Phyllis.

After a day spent going to Molly's future employer with her, which went very well, he left the next morning to get back to work. Molly seemed genuinely grateful that he'd come to her aid and her manner towards him had much improved. She kissed his cheek as he left.

Tom arrived back at the yard at about five o'clock on Tuesday evening. Ed saw him come in and ran over to speak to him.

"Where've you been?" he said. "Everyone's been looking for you. Jake said you'd left. The Mistress is going frantic! I think she's real cross. She's in a foul mood."

"Didn't Jake tell you I had to see my daughter urgently?" asked Tom. "I told him I'd be back as soon as I could."

But it seems that only half of the message had got through. Jake told them all that Tom had gone, but not much more than that. Just then Phyllis came out and saw him.

"Tom Finnimore!" she shouted. "Where have you been? Come and see me at once!"

Tom followed her up to the house dejectedly. Once there, she turned on him angrily, but he could see she'd been crying.

"What the hell do you think you've been playing at?" she cried. "Going off like that! Do you think you can just get your job back again, when you come back? Do you have an explanation?"

"Yes!" said Tom. "I told Jake. My daughter, Molly, needed me urgently and I had to go to Bristol the next day. I told the boy that I'd be back as soon as possible and to let you know. Unfortunately, I think he might have been a bit the worse for wear. I'm sorry if the message didn't get through, but it was very late on Saturday night and I didn't want to disturb you. If I hadn't left then, I would have missed the train."

"Why didn't you leave a note?" she demanded, but her tone had softened slightly.

"Because I can't write!" said Tom. "Not even my own name. I'm sorry."

Phyllis turned away from him and then suddenly burst out crying.

"Oh Tom!" she said. "I thought I'd lost you. I thought you'd left because of me. Please don't do that again. I can't bear to be without you! I love you!"

Tom took her gently in his arms, stroking away her tears and soothing her pain, before kissing her again and again. They spent a long time in each other's arms before they finally sat down together by the fire, happier than they'd ever been.

"So what now?" asked Tom. "What shall we tell everyone?"

"I suggest we try and keep this discreet," answered Phyllis. "We obviously can't deny what we feel for each other, but maybe we can keep it from other people for a while. What do you think?"

Tom agreed it might be best for the time being, although he felt he really wanted to tell the whole world because he was so happy.

Chapter 23

The dark days of winter eventually gave way to the fresh brightness of spring, and Tom and Phyllis were as happy as ever. Tom spent most evenings over at the house and often did not appear back at his cottage until just before he needed to get ready for work. His bed was rarely slept in and who could blame him? He had found a level of love and happiness he had never thought possible. They were good for each other. Phyllis made Tom feel strong and confident, whereas he allowed her to be vulnerable for a change. Phyllis had spent the last year desperately trying to be strong for her family and now it was her turn to be looked after and cherished.

The only thing that slightly marred Tom's happiness was the fact that he couldn't tell anyone. At Easter that year, he invited his son John down to stay with him and to his joy, the lad accepted. John was about to start work after Easter, in a new, slightly better paid job as a labourer, so this seemed the perfect opportunity for him to have a short 'holiday' in Farncombe. Tom wanted him to get to know Phyllis, but he didn't mention this when he invited him as he didn't want to cause any problems.

Young John arrived on the day before Good Friday, his face beaming as his father met him off the train. His hair was a lighter brown than Tom's and flopped untidily over his eyes. He had turned into a sensible young man who was keen to get on in the world of work. He had not yet experienced the joys and pangs of love, but, Tom thought as he looked at him, it wouldn't be long. John was on the verge of manhood.

The days they spent together that Easter were a joy. John stayed in the cottage with Tom, eating at the big house and even accompanying him to the yard on Saturday. The men were only too happy to see John and they teased Tom for keeping quiet about having had children.

"You're a dark horse!" exclaimed Ed. "Didn't even know you'd been married."

"Oh well," laughed Tom. "There's a lot you don't know about me." *How true that was*, he thought.

Young John enjoyed seeing all the facets of the tanning industry even though the work didn't appeal to him. He marvelled at the quality of the finished leather and at all the effort that went into it.

On Good Friday, the two of them went to church, then afterwards explored Godalming together. Tom delighted in showing his son all his favourite haunts. The weather was fine that afternoon and they enjoyed a leisurely stroll by the river and around the town.

More than this, however, Tom loved seeing John getting to know Phyllis, talking and laughing quite naturally with her. Of course, Tom didn't spend his usual amount of time over at the house whilst his son was around, but on Friday evening Phyllis invited them both to stay on after supper for the rest of the evening. Phyllis kindly got them both some ales and made them welcome. She spent a lot of time talking to John about his plans for the future. John liked her immediately because she treated him like an adult, not a child.

After an enjoyable evening, as they were walking back to the cottage, John said to Tom, "I can understand why you like Phyllis so much, Dad. She's so easy to be with. I'm sorry I didn't want to meet her. I was just being stupid. There's no reason why you shouldn't be friends with her."

Tom then braved a question. "What if we were more than that?" he asked. "Would you mind?"

John frowned and thought for a moment, and Tom wished he'd kept quiet, but then the young man said, "No Dad. I'd rather you were happy. After all, Mum's been gone a couple of years now, and you had a miserable time with her anyway. I'm not stupid. I can see what she did to you. You did your best."

Tom felt suddenly overcome with emotion, turned to the boy and hugged him briefly. "Thanks" was all he could say. Then they moved on.

On Sunday at church, however, things developed in a direction Tom would rather they hadn't. He'd decided to go to Farncombe again that week in the hope of introducing his son to

134

Phyllis' children. He had his chance after the service and moved in to speak to them. Some polite introductions were made and Caroline, the married daughter, expressed her satisfaction at seeing Tom with his son. Things were going well, thought Tom. However, during the service, a collection had been made for the Prisoners Aid Society and afterwards comments were made on this.

Young Fliss said, "I feel it is a very good thing to help the unfortunates in this world."

Tom winced.

"Yes," replied Caroline. "Everyone makes mistakes and deserves a second chance."

Her mother smiled knowingly and Tom felt himself going red. Unfortunately, his son John had no idea that they didn't know about his father's past and enthusiastically added, "Yes, they really helped Dad when he got out. He'd have had nothing otherwise."

"What do you mean – 'got out'?" asked Caroline, a look of horror on her face.

"Well, out of Millbank prison, of course," answered John. "It *was* there, wasn't it Dad?"

Everyone turned to look at Tom and he turned crimson.

"Yes," he muttered.

"You mean you are an ex-convict?" exclaimed Fliss. "Mother, did you know?"

"Yes!" replied her mother. "And it doesn't worry me one bit."

"Gosh!" exclaimed William, sounding impressed. "That's great. What did you do?"

"It's not something to be proud of, William!" said Caroline sternly. "I'm ashamed of you Mother, associating with criminals. Aren't you scared he'll rob or murder you or something? I've heard they always go back to crime again."

"Don't be ridiculous!" replied Phyllis. "Tom's an honest, hard-working man. Wasn't it you who said everyone deserves a second chance?"

"That's all well and good," Caroline retorted. "But they don't have to come 'round here!" She turned to Tom. "I don't want you anywhere near my family. James, bring the baby. We're going home." With that she turned and marched off.

"Wait for me!" cried her sister, Fliss. "I'm not staying here to consort with criminals."

They all left and there was an awkward silence for a few moments.

"Oh, crikey!" said Tom's son, John. "I'm sorry, Dad. I thought they knew and that's why they were talking like that. Why are they so two-faced? No offence meant!" he added to Phyllis.

"It's okay," she said. "None taken. You're right, they are two-faced."

Her son Jack now piped up suddenly. "Well, I don't care, Tom! I like you and that's all there is to it."

"Me too!" said William. "Without you I wouldn't be doing what I am now."

Throughout most of this exchange, Tom had hardly uttered a word. Now he spoke up.

"Look, lads," he said, "Caroline's right in a way. It's certainly nothing to be proud of and that's why I never said anything about it, except to your Ma." He looked at Phyllis. "I'm really sorry they're upset about it."

"They'll just have to get over it!" she declared. "Let's go home for tea."

The rest of John's stay was uneventful, although the incident left an unpleasant taint in the air. When John left to go home, he hugged his father and wished him well, sending his best wishes to Phyllis and her family. If anything, the admiration of Phyllis' two sons for Tom had increased, but he felt uneasy. He didn't want to break up her family, but he knew that opinion about him was divided.

A few weeks later, however, a new employee started at the yard and Phyllis suggested that due to 'lack of room', Tom should move into a spare room of the main house with her, then the new man could have the cottage.

"Are you sure?" Tom asked her privately, when she put the idea to him. "I don't want to make things worse with your daughters."

She reassured him that it was only their own happiness that mattered and so Tom moved in. Ostensibly, he had his own bedroom, but it was never slept in. To all intents and purposes, they were living as 'man and wife'. Phyllis' younger son Jack, (who was the only one still living at home) just accepted Tom around as a normal part of proceedings and made no comment on it. Luckily, the older children rarely visited the family home these days. Ed and some of the men from the yard sniggered a bit, but nobody really cared. Tom and Phyllis were good people and deserved to be happy. Everyone turned a blind eye.

Tom knew he wanted to be with Phyllis for the rest of his life. There was no doubting that. One day, he plucked up the courage to ask her to marry him.

Nervously he began, "Phyll, you know what I feel about you. There'll never be anyone else for me. I really think we should get married. We get on so well together. I know we've both had families in the past and we won't start a new one now, but I just want to be able to tell everyone you're mine. I'm proud of it and I want it to be permanent. What do you say, Phyll? Please."

She smiled at him, but there was sadness in her eyes as well.

"Of course I'll marry you some day, Tom. It's all I want as well, but not just yet. I'd like my girls to come to terms with it all and accept you. I know it's hard, waiting, but we're alright as we are now, aren't we?"

Tom was disappointed, but knew how much Phyllis loved her children and how upset she'd been about the recent rift between them.

"I understand," he said, holding her close. "But let's not wait too long. We're not getting any younger, you know!"

The subject was dropped for the time being, but Tom still longed to marry her.

To her credit, Phyllis did invite the two daughters over, with the idea of getting them to know Tom better, but they refused to come. She no longer saw them at church on Sunday as they had taken to attending another parish. They made excuses that it was more convenient but Phyllis knew they were avoiding the area, in case they saw Tom. She still visited them at their homes and she did her best to persuade them of Tom's good character, but unfortunately, they refused to listen.

Chapter 24

One evening in September, Phyllis seemed very quiet at dinner. She looked pale and worried, and after everyone else had left, Tom asked her what was wrong.

"Are you alright?" he said concerned. "You don't look well."

"Tom, we need to talk," she replied. "We've got a serious problem. I don't know what to do. I think I'm pregnant!"

"What?" cried Tom. "But you can't be! Surely we're too old for that sort of thing? We're in our forties." He was shocked.

"I know," said Phyllis. "I can't believe it myself. What are we going to do?"

They sat there in stunned silence for a few minutes, thinking. There were so few options for unmarried mothers then, although being recently widowed would maybe mean that Phyllis would be able to hide the shame. There were back street abortions, (but they were highly dangerous), otherwise the Foundling Hospital often took illegitimate babies away (forcibly) from their mothers, causing untold suffering.

"Well," said Tom, "this means we really should get married for the sake of the baby at least. You know I want to marry you anyway. No one can possibly object to it now!"

"But they'll say we're only getting married for the baby!" she protested. "And I don't want anyone to say that. I want them to know we love each other and that this is the only reason we're getting married. I'm not even sure I can cope with a baby again now, after all this time. You probably don't want it either."

The tears poured down her face and Tom held her tightly to comfort her.

"Dearest Phyllis," he said. "Don't get me wrong. I think it's wonderful! It's an opportunity to have a new family for us, one of our own. I had very little involvement with my children last time, as you know, and this would be a fantastic second chance for me. This time I could be a real father. It was just a bit of a shock, that's all. Please marry me and we'll make everything work out, together."

"I need to talk to my children," Phyllis murmured tearfully. "If they can accept it, then we'll get married. I don't know what I'll do if they don't. I can't go against them, I really can't."

Tom wasn't present when Phyllis spoke to her family that weekend, but she was crying when she returned so he knew it wasn't good news.

"What happened?" he asked. "How did it go?"

"The boys were okay about it," she told him, between sobs. "Much as I thought, but Caroline and Phyllis say that they will never see or speak to me again if I marry you. They say you took advantage of me and that you should be sent away or even arrested! I told them I love you but they don't understand. They just see you as an 'ex-con' I'm afraid, and they said they are prepared to tell everybody, including all the men in the yard. They don't want me, or the baby, to have your name. They even want me to give it away."

Tom sighed. He knew his past was a problem but he hadn't anticipated this.

Phyllis continued, "I tried to explain that you were very young when it all happened, that you'd been married since and looked after your wife when she was dying, but it all made things worse. They said you are just a thief, who drove his wife to drink and that you would do the same to me. They said criminals always return to crime. I'm sorry Tom. If I marry you now, they are threatening to have you arrested on a charge of rape or seduction! We can't risk that. I really feel Caroline would go through with it. She is so angry."

Tom felt scared. It was common for men, at that time, to be arrested and jailed for seducing or molesting women, no matter what the circumstances. Even though Tom knew Phyllis would speak up for him, with his previous record it was unlikely that anyone would believe the truth, especially with a pregnancy involved. If the two daughters collaborated against him, he wouldn't have much chance.

"You're not going to send me away, are you?" he asked anxiously. "I couldn't bear it! I'd rather be arrested than that."

"Of course not!" replied Phyllis. "I couldn't do that. The only thing I can think is that we keep everything as quiet as possible. If I stay away from the yard and don't go out, maybe I can hide my condition." She paused. "Unless you want me to get rid of it, that is?" She looked anxiously at him.

"No, of course not!" Tom exclaimed. "It's our child and I'd like to be its father. Unless *you* don't want it, of course?" he added doubtfully.

Phyllis threw her arms around him suddenly. "Oh, I hoped you'd say that!" she cried. "I really want our baby, whatever happens. I'll stay away from Caroline and Fliss as much as possible, and get a nurse in to help me when I need it. The less I have to do with the girls, the better."

"I don't want you to be shamed and known as a 'fallen woman'," Tom said. "Not just because of me. I'm sorry, Phyllis, really I am!"

"Tom dearest," she replied gently. "I'm not ashamed of our love and I'm not sorry about the baby either, so please remember that. We can get through this together."

They embraced and were closer than ever. Nothing could tear them apart.

So Phyllis wrapped herself in a voluminous cloak and loose clothing, and became more or less house-bound for the next few months. Tom told everyone at the yard that she wasn't well and that she needed to rest indoors, and they seemed to accept it. The men still came over for supper at the house, but respected her privacy and did not intrude. Her two sons spent more time with her, William visiting at weekends whenever he could and helping out where needed. Phyllis was no longer attending church on Sundays now, staying well away from prying eyes and her daughters' disapproval. Jack, of course, lived at home as well, although he attended school during the week, and Tom was there in the evenings, so she wasn't all alone. When the nights became darker but the weather was still mild, he and Phyllis managed a few short walks around the local area to give her a chance to get out and have some fresh air. They avoided people and only went out at night when they couldn't be seen.

Phyllis's pregnancy progressed well and she bloomed, in spite of her maturity. Her daughters stayed away and did not visit, for which they were both grateful, although Tom knew Phyllis was sad inside. He wondered if he should try to talk to them and attempt a reconciliation, but thought it would probably be a mistake. They'd heard, via William, that Caroline's opinion was set as hard as ever, and that she'd said if she saw Tom with her mother, she would call the local constable. So discretion was certainly the order of the day.

Tom knew he needed to speak to his own family about the situation, before long. He dreaded telling his son John, but he knew he had to be honest with him. The following Sunday, therefore, he made his regular visit up to Bermondsey. He arrived at Dick and Eliza's house nervously. John was no longer living there, as he now had lodgings of his own just around the corner. He'd been working six months now and had even started seeing a young local girl he'd met. Tom wanted to speak to his older brother, Dick, privately first to get some advice.

"Dick," he began. "I really need to talk to you. I've got a problem and I need some advice."

Dick could see Tom was worried. "What's wrong, little brother?" he said. "Tell me all about it."

"Well, it's all to do with the woman at the yard, who I've got very close to."

"Phyllis?" asked Dick and Tom nodded. "John told me that you're in love with her."

"Really?" said Tom. "But I hadn't actually told him that."

"You didn't need to!" Dick laughed. "It's obvious just from looking at you. You never stop talking about her. I've never seen you so happy."

"Well, the problem is, she's pregnant," revealed Tom.

"Oh Tom, really!" exclaimed Dick. "Couldn't you have got married first?"

"Well I asked her, but her daughters don't approve of me, so we waited and now this has happened."

"Can't you marry her now?" asked Dick.

"No, her daughters know about my time in prison and they're threatening to have me convicted of rape or something. We're trying to keep it all quiet, but what I really wanted advice on is how to tell John about it."

"Well," replied Dick thoughtfully. "He already knows you love her and he said how much he likes her, so I'd just be honest with him. He deserves it after all. He's a mature young man. I'm sure he'll come to terms with it."

"What do you think he'll say? Do you think he'll reject me?" asked Tom.

But Dick had no answers for that and told Tom he just had to go and see John for himself.

John, as always, was pleased to see his father, but after a bit of general chat Tom broached the subject of Phyllis. The young man enthusiastically asked after her, and that is when Tom blurted out the truth. "She's fine, John, but I'm afraid she's pregnant!"

There was a silence for a minute or two and Tom feared the worst.

"Dad, what were you thinking? How could you do this?"

"I didn't mean to," said Tom apologetically. "Please don't think this makes you any less to me. You'll always be my dear son."

"I'm not worried about that!" cried John, "I know that! I was just thinking about poor Phyllis!"

Tom felt so relieved. He'd imagined John would be jealous or hostile. He reassured the lad that he loved Phyllis, was looking after her and was keen to marry her as soon as possible.

"It's her daughters that are the problem," he explained. "But they'll come 'round sooner or later."

"I do hope so, Dad," said John. "I'd love to see you two get married. It's very exciting to think that I will have a new brother or sister quite soon."

Chapter 25

Tom and Phyllis' baby was born in 1861, with only a solitary nurse present to support the birth. Phyllis went into labour just before dawn one frosty morning in February. Tom rushed downstairs, dressing hastily and waking her son, Jack. They were all prepared and had a plan of action worked out in advance. Jack dressed and then went to fetch the nurse from the village whilst Tom looked after Phyllis, soothing her and trying to ease the pain. When Jack came back with the nurse then Tom rushed down to the yard to tell them he wouldn't be in that day. He told Ed that Phyllis was ill and needed looking after. Ed smiled. He knew the truth.

"So the baby's coming at last!" he said. "Well, wish her all the best from me."

Tom stared at him, surprised. "I don't know what you mean," he blustered.

"Oh come off it, mate," said Ed. "I've been through it meself five times. I can see the signs. I ain't daft you know!"

"Oh well," stammered Tom. "Well, thanks."

"We all think it's great, you and 'er together," Ed continued. "Nice to see 'er so happy again. Go on, get off with you and look after 'er."

Tom thanked him again and sped off to find Bill, a reliable man from the yard, to deliver three ready prepared notes to William, Caroline and Fliss. These were informing them of the impending delivery and expressing the wish that they would come and see her as soon as they could. Tom knew William would come as soon as he could leave work for the day, but he didn't hold out much hope for the girls. When Phyllis wrote the notes she told Tom how much she wanted them to set aside their differences and visit, but they both knew it was a forlorn hope.

Tom returned to the house and tried to be useful, but there was nothing he could do. Tom and Jack spent most of the time pacing up and down, talking and drinking tea. The nurse wouldn't let them near. At about 3 o'clock in the afternoon, they finally heard the sound of a baby crying and they both let out a cheer. Phyllis had had a beautiful baby son and all was well.

As soon as he could, Tom rushed to Phyllis' bedside. She looked exhausted but happy.

"It's a boy, Tom," she told him. "He's beautiful! Look, over there. Go and hold him."

Tom picked up the bawling infant and cradled him gently, marvelling at the miracle of newborn life. He felt a surge of pure love for the child. To think that this small bundle was his and Phyllis' child! It was amazing.

"What shall we call him?" he asked, expecting Phyllis to have her own ideas.

But she was open to discussion, unlike Mary Ann, and they settled on Joseph James. Tom hesitantly suggested the name Joseph, after his friend in Millbank prison, and found Phyllis liked it as well. Unfortunately, the baby could not be registered as a Finnimore as they weren't married, and so he was put down on the records as a Stedman, much to Tom's disappointment.

"We really need to get married," he said. "Can't we talk to the girls again? Maybe if they saw the baby they'd change their minds."

As expected, William came over after work and spent all evening there, but the girls didn't appear. This made Phyllis very sad, and the next day he found her crying due to their rejection. This made him determined to speak to them if he could, to try and persuade them to visit at least. He decided his best chance was to speak to the younger girl, Fliss, as her opinions might be more flexible.

The next day, he arrived at the vicarage where Fliss was working and asked to see her. He was shown into a little parlour and a few minutes later, she appeared. Her reaction was hostile.

"What are *you* doing here?"

Tom held up his hand to silence her. "I need to talk to you," he said. "So please hear me out. Did you know your mother gave birth to a baby boy this week, without any help or support from her two daughters?"

His tone was angry and Fliss hung her head in shame at first, but then retorted defensively, "Well you shouldn't have got her pregnant then!"

"Well," replied Tom. "I asked her to marry me months ago and you know what she said? She said she'd love to but she didn't want to upset you two, so she wanted to wait. Now look what's happened! This is all your fault for being so disapproving."

"Is it any wonder when you're a criminal?" Fliss hit back.

"Listen to me!" Tom responded defiantly. "I was pardoned by Lord Melbourne himself, the prime minister of England. Do you really think I can be such a bad person if he pardoned me?"

She wasn't sure what to say and so Tom continued. "How old are you?"

"Sixteen, but what's that got to do with it?"

"I was your age when it all happened. Yes, I was stupid but I was very young. I'd had a row with my girlfriend and went out drinking with a mate. I was so drunk I didn't even know what I was doing! It was only a few chickens and yet I was sentenced to seven years transportation. My family appealed and they reduced it to imprisonment, but it was hard. When you say 'criminals return to crime', do you really know what you're talking about? Would I *really* want to spend more time on the stinking hulks with hundreds of other men, in a rat-infested ship, beaten by the guards and kept in chains? Because that's what it's really like. Then again, would I *really* want to go back to Millbank to exist in solitary confinement, unable to speak a word for fear of punishment? The answer is 'No!' Of course not. Three years was enough for me, I can tell you."

"Well, it's not just about that!" declared Fliss. "What about your wife and children? You treated them very badly."

Tom laughed bitterly.

"Me, treated them badly! I like that. My wife, Mary Ann, ran up debts everywhere, then when I tried to stop her she left me and took the children with her. I didn't even know where they were for years. Then she takes up with another man, a drunk, who gets her into it as well. Years later, when he dies she suddenly appears back to see me, begging my forgiveness and asking for help."

He paused, remembering the pain, then continued more gently, "Unfortunately, it was all too late. I nursed her through her last illness until the end. It was all I could do. I've tried since then to form a new relationship with my children. They didn't even know me, so it's been hard. I really want the chance to be a father again. I lost that, before. Are you going to deny me this?"

Fliss shook her head, her eyes misty.

"More than that," continued Tom, "I understand that you hate me, but do you hate your mother?"

"No, of course not!" she replied.

"Well, why are you treating her like this?" he asked indignantly. "She's given up so much for you over the last year or so, and now you've abandoned her. At the very least, you could go and visit her. You could also talk to Caroline and try to persuade her."

"I will try," she murmured.

"Well, that's good," said Tom. "But I tell you one thing – I love your mother and I want to marry her. There is no way you are going to keep me away from her. We will always be together, whether you like it or not! That's all I have to say."

He turned to leave, but Fliss said, "Mr Finnimore – Tom! I'm sorry. I didn't understand. I'll try and make things better and I'll go and see Mother."

He gazed at her. "I hope so," he said. "I really do."

Fliss was as good as her word and visited her mother that Sunday after church. Tom kept out the way at first so as not to spoil anything, and there were many hugs and a few tears (Of Caroline, however, there was still no sign). Tom came in later that afternoon to see mother, daughter and his new baby all happily ensconced together in the front room.

"Tom," called Phyllis. "Come and have tea with us."

He hesitated but Fliss added, "Yes, please do."

She smiled at him and he realised that she had accepted him at last.

"Joe's a beautiful baby," she said. "You're both very lucky."

"How is Caroline?" he asked nervously.

"Well," she replied. "She's planning to visit in a week or two. I think she's slowly coming 'round. I did talk to her and I'm hopeful, that's all I can say. It's difficult to tell with her, she keeps things very close to her chest."

That night Phyllis and Tom lay snuggled up together in bed with baby Joe. They were warm and cosy, and Phyllis was very happy.

"Tom," she said. "I know I have you to thank for changing Fliss' opinion. You're a brave and wonderful man! I know it took a lot of effort to do that and I'm very grateful."

"Your happiness is all that counts to me," he told her, and held her tight. "Sooner or later, we'll be able to be together properly."

He hoped this was true, but felt doubtful about Caroline.

A couple of weeks later, however, the oldest daughter *did* pay a visit to her mother, one weekday afternoon, whilst Tom was at work. Phyllis was delighted to see her, but it wasn't an emotional reunion. Caroline was frosty but polite. She stayed long enough to take tea and admire the baby, but the afternoon was stiff and awkward. When Phyllis mentioned Tom, Caroline refused to talk about him.

"I cannot discuss *that* man!" she declared. "My feelings are the same as ever."

Phyllis left well alone, and was happy when Caroline appeared again a couple of weeks later. This time her attitude seemed a little softer and so Phyllis invited her to come over for a day at Easter. Surprisingly, Caroline agreed, but emphasised that she would not want to see or talk to Tom.

"I do not wish to have anything to do with him, Mother. I hope that's clear!"

Phyllis apologised to Tom about this, but was slightly encouraged by the fact that her daughter was, at least, visiting now.

"I'm sure things will change soon," Phyllis assured him. "She's just got too much pride to back down."

April came and the weather was steadily improving. Green shoots were poking out here and there and the days, although still cold at times, were brighter. Baby Joe grew strongly, and Phyllis had recovered her health and strength. She had started taking Joe out in a pram for walks on sunnier days, ignoring the stares and whispers of the local community. Tom usually went out with her on Sundays. He was very proud of his fine son and saw no reason to be ashamed.

At Easter that year, Caroline visited as promised with her baby daughter Anne, now a toddler and into everything. Tom had felt a sense of foreboding at the forthcoming visit and, although it was a holiday, he volunteered to stay well out of the way. He decided to take himself off down by the River Wey on the far bank, which was quiet and peaceful. Not many people used that side as the paths were narrow, rough and a bit overgrown. Tom preferred it as it reminded him of his childhood in Devon. He strolled along, trying to enjoy the loveliness of the day and the flow of the river, but he had an uneasy feeling, which just wouldn't shift. He sat down to rest a while in the shade.

Just then, across the river on the other bank, he saw Phyllis and Caroline walking along with the two youngest children followed by son Jack, trailing along quite a way behind. The other bank had a better, more level path, ideally suited to the pram that Phyllis was pushing. Little Anne was toddling along happily, refusing to hold her mother's hand, running backwards and forwards frequently. Tom reckoned he was safe enough to watch them from this distance, and hopefully Caroline wouldn't even notice him. He smiled to see the two mothers chatting happily. Things seemed to be going well. A cloud suddenly hid the sun for a moment, dimming the light and making him shiver. He sat up to try to get warm. Just then he heard a splash and a scream and looked up to see that little Anne had fallen in the water. There was a scene of utter panic on the far side. The current was quite fast there and Tom could see Anne being swept away. Caroline was screaming and Phyllis was chasing along the bank, desperately trying to grab the child, but she was too far away. No one seemed to know what to do. Tom took all this in, in an instant, although it was a moment that seemed to last forever. Then, without stopping to think twice, he threw off his heavy boots and jacket, which would have weighed him down, and dived in. He had learnt to swim early on when playing in the Alphin Brook as a child, then later in the River Exe. Although he hadn't been swimming in years, it was a skill never forgotten. He swam across, fighting the current, to get to the little girl. The river was so fast here it was like wading through treacle. She was struggling now, going under occasionally and crying in panic. Tom was having a job to catch up with her. Luckily, some vegetation in the river slowed her down just long enough for him to reach her. He grabbed her and pulled her upwards, keeping her above the surface, then he swam slowly and with much effort to the bank where Phyllis was waiting to take her from him. Caroline was hysterical. Phyllis returned Anne to her, saying sternly, "Pull yourself together, Caroline!"

Then she returned to help Tom out. "Tom!" she cried. "You were so brave. Come and get dry and warm. You must be frozen!"

Now that the adrenaline rush had gone Tom felt shaky and cold. His legs felt like jelly and he could hardly stand. Phyllis took charge of the whole situation, sending Caroline on ahead to the house with Anne, getting Jack to fetch Tom's coat and boots, and taking Tom and Joe slowly home with her. Tom leant on her arm most of the way as he felt so wobbly.

They returned to the house and Phyllis organised dry clothes and hot drinks for everyone who needed them. Caroline was upstairs with Anne, who apparently was none the worse for her ordeal. Tom sat by the fire shivering. It took him a long time to get warm. The cold water had chilled him to the bone. The Doctor was called and pronounced little Anne quite well but in need of a good rest. He also prescribed a sedative for Caroline and checked out Tom, but declared he was fine. Caroline and Anne stayed upstairs so Tom rested in the parlour by the fire, wrapped in a blanket. He didn't even realise he was nodding off, but he awoke some time later to find Caroline coming into the room. He started up, ready to leave but much to his surprise, Caroline flung herself down at his feet.

"Mr Finnimore, please don't go! I've come to beg your forgiveness. I've been so wrong. You are a good and decent man and you saved my little girl's life. I can never thank you enough!"

Tom looked at her doubtfully. "If that's the only reason you think I'm good and decent," he said, "what's to stop you changing your mind later and having me arrested?"

"Please, Mr Finnimore," she pleaded. "I know I've been stupid and cruel. My sister told me the truth, but I wouldn't listen. I was too proud. I'm sorry! I can only beg you to give me another chance. Please!"

She gazed up at him, tears in her eyes and he felt she really meant what she said. He took both her hands in his.

"What about your mother?" he asked, looking straight into her eyes. "I love her and I want to marry her. What do you say about that?"

"I'd be happy for you to marry her," she replied. "I know what I said before, but that was just because I loved my father so much and I couldn't face seeing my mother with someone else! I'm sorry. I was being selfish. She deserves to be happy and so do you."

Tom raised Caroline up onto a seat beside him, saying, "I'm delighted to hear that! Let's start again as friends this time."

They hugged and Caroline let out all her pent up emotions in floods of tears. He soothed her gently until her sobs subsided.

Tom then went to Phyllis and told her about his reconciliation with Caroline. She was overjoyed.

"Now, Phyllis," he said seriously. "Will you marry me at last? There's nothing in our way now. Please!"

"Oh Tom, of course I will!" she replied happily. "I've been waiting for this day for so long. Let's set a date right away!"

That night there was a joyful celebration. Caroline, John, William and Fliss all joined them for supper and everyone toasted the happy couple. At last, they could look forward to better times.

Chapter 26

Tom and Phyllis got married on Sunday 25th August 1861 at St Mary the Virgin church in Shalford. Phyllis chose Shalford because she'd grown up there and it was a beautiful church, very high and grand for such a small village. It had been newly built in 1847 and so had a freshness and lightness to it, unlike many of the dark and gloomy buildings of the past. They waited until August, although they would have preferred sooner, just to make sure that as many of their respective children and family members could get there as possible.

In the few months beforehand, Tom got to know some of Phyllis' siblings. Her younger brother William was a bargeman like their father before him, and so was often away, but Tom met his wife Emma and their children. They were kind and welcoming, and it felt good to be accepted as part of the family. Phyllis' sisters, Caroline and Mary, were quite a bit younger than Phyllis and so were also busy raising families. Because of the age difference they weren't particularly close, but they were happy for Phyllis and keen to come to the wedding. They knew how lonely she'd been in recent years. Tom also got Phyllis to write to his family in Devon and was delighted that Lizzie, her husband Daniel and his youngest brother Eddie would all be coming up. He had always been close to Lizzie and was looking forward to seeing her again. She wrote that she was so pleased that he had found happiness again. She, more than anyone, knew how much he had suffered. John, as always, was tied to the shop. He couldn't afford to lose trade by closing for a few days. The living was too precarious for that. Tom understood. Dick, Eliza, Will and Ann were all going to be attending, and Tom took Phyllis up to Bermondsey beforehand so they could meet. They got on very well, Phyllis and Eliza spending ages chatting about domestic details. Everyone admired Phyllis' good sense and calm stability. She was like a rock that turbulent water just flowed around. Dick told Tom he was a lucky man.

"She'll keep you on the straight and narrow!" he teased. "She's a strong woman, that one."

Tom laughingly agreed, although knew privately another more vulnerable side to her, which he loved and cherished.

All their children from their previous marriages had also agreed to come, and Tom was very pleased to hear that Caroline had agreed to be one of the witnesses. Her attitude and opinion certainly *had* changed for the better. Tom's ex-sister in law, Hannah, was even going to come from Bristol with his daughter Molly, so it was set to be a real celebration. His son, John had also proudly agreed to be his best man, which made Tom even happier.

The day was fine and sunny as everyone gathered at the church. The sun shone through the stained glass windows casting beautiful rainbow coloured patterns on the floor. Phyllis wore her best dress of pale grey striped silk, with white flowers in her hair, which was dressed elegantly up on top. Her younger daughter Fliss had helped her to get ready on the day. She looked very lovely, thought Tom as he saw her approach up the aisle. When they were side by side he squeezed her hand gently and whispered in her ear. "You look beautiful! I love you."

She glowed with happiness and he did as well. He had his best dark suit on for the occasion and looked very smart.

They made their vows solemnly, gazing deep into each other's eyes. There was nothing that Tom had ever wanted more than this. He felt so proud to be marrying this woman.

The bells rang out as they left the church, and friends and family couldn't wait to congratulate them. The party afterwards at the local alehouse, The Seahorse Inn, was full of love and warmth. Lizzie hugged and kissed them both.

"Tom, you rascal!" she teased when she saw baby Joe. "Started a family already – well, I never! Seriously Tom, I think it's great and you deserve to be happy. We all hope you'll come and visit us in Devon some time."

That night, Tom and Phyllis lay wrapped in each other's arms. Though they had made love many times before, this time felt different somehow.

"It feels so right," said Tom, trying to put it into words.

Phyllis smiled up at him. "I know what you mean," she said. "It's the way things were meant to be."

On the morning of December 15th 1861, Tom and Phyllis awoke to the sound of church bells tolling out mournfully across the countryside. They jumped out of bed anxiously and peered out the window. There seemed to be a general hubbub and panic below. Were they at war again, or was it something else? They rushed downstairs to find out. The news was very sad – Prince Albert had died of the typhoid and the whole country was in mourning.

The next few days were very gloomy, as was Christmas that year. Shops were shut, windows shuttered and people wore black out of respect. Even the poorer classes, like themselves, were affected by it. Work continued in the yard, but no trade took place with other people, only day to day, routine activities, mostly carried out in a grim silence. Flags were at half-mast and Christmas was a sombre affair. The usual celebrations, which Prince Albert had done so much to popularise, were kept to an absolute minimum. It was rumoured that the Queen had gone into total seclusion in her grief, and the nation felt for her.

Despite this, 1862 dawned bright and full of promise for Tom and Phyllis. They had been happily married for six months now, and baby Joe was fast approaching his first birthday. He was a happy, healthy child who always seemed to be smiling. Tom's only regret was that his son wasn't registered as a 'Finnimore'. He happened to mention this to Ed one day, when discussing their respective families. Ed, in his usual easygoing manner, laughed and told him not to be so daft.

"Just have him baptised by the vicar, all proper like," he said. "Then he'll be yours right enough. It don't signify what the law says. In front of the Almighty he'll be a Finnimore and that's all that matters."

Tom wondered why he had never thought of this before and rushed off to put it into practice. Phyllis agreed it was an excellent idea and they set a date around the time of Joe's birthday in February.

The baptism took place at St Johns Church in Farncombe, conducted by the Reverend Charles Dallas. He was a kindly man who was happy to advise Tom and Phyllis on the procedure and requirements. They chose three godparents for little Joe – Ed, because of his helpfulness and general good humour, Phyllis' younger sister, Caroline and Tom's brother, Dick, from Bermondsey in order to represent both families. It was a small and simple affair, with just a few local friends and family, but it meant a lot to Tom. When he heard Joe's full name and surname read out in the church, he felt choked with emotion. Phyllis saw his face and squeezed his hand in a reassuring manner. Tom smiled. She was always there for him.

Afterwards, everyone came back to their house for tea and cakes. They had managed to lay on a good spread and it was a very pleasant afternoon. Tom felt happy that his son, at last, had his name.

Chapter 27

In April that year, Phyllis surprised Tom by announcing she was pregnant again. He was delighted, but also a bit concerned. After all, she was nearly 45 years old and the dangers of childbirth were great enough at any age. However, he told himself that she'd been well enough all through her last pregnancy with Joe, so hopefully there was no need to worry. He still couldn't shake that nagging feeling, though.

In June that year, Phyllis began to feel ill. It was a beautiful sunny day and she'd been outside a lot, working on the garden they had, which grew vegetables for the household. She suddenly developed a blinding headache and could hardly see. Her vision was blurred, with flashing lights in front of her eyes. Somehow, she staggered inside, thinking it was too much sun. When Tom got in from work later, he found her lying on the couch, in the dark, hardly able to move.

"Tom," she called. "Help me! I'm frightened. I can't see properly!"

After helping her up to bed, he rushed off to get the doctor, despite her protests that it was just a touch of sunstroke. When the doctor came, however, he found her blood pressure to be dangerously high and was very concerned. After Dr Smith had seen her, he came down to talk to Tom.

"I'm afraid she has a condition known as pre-eclampsia," he told him.

"What on earth is that?" Tom exclaimed, very alarmed.

"Basically, she has very high blood pressure and lots of toxins in her urine due to the pregnancy. It's her age, unfortunately."

"What do you mean by 'toxins'?" asked Tom, anxiously.

"It means her body is getting poisoned," the doctor explained. "And it's very dangerous for both her and the baby."

"But you can do something for her, can't you? She'll be alright, won't she?" he cried.

"I hope so," said the doctor. "But the only thing we can do now is to give her complete bed rest. It's her best chance. She may also get pains in her stomach, and her face and hands may swell up, so be prepared for it. I'll visit regularly and monitor her. I also have a medicine which might help. I'll get some sent over."

"What about the baby?" Tom asked. "Will it be alright?"

"It'll probably be quite small and weak," said the doctor. "And we may have to induce labour early, so I can't say for sure I'm afraid. All your wife's symptoms should go as soon as she's had the baby, so the sooner the better. You must keep her calm and rested in the meantime."

"But why has this happened?" questioned Tom. "She didn't have any problems with the last baby."

"Sometimes, it just happens," the doctor told him. "But it's more common with age. I would advise her not to have any more after this."

Phyllis' visions and headache had cleared for the time being and she was keen to get up, but was firmly told that she must stay in bed. She protested vigorously at this, as she was an active person who hated being idle.

"But there's the garden to see to," she said. "And who's going to cook for the men? I can't just stay in bed all the time."

"You must," replied the doctor sternly, "if you value your life and that of your baby. It's that serious, I'm afraid."

At this, Phyllis gave in, seeing sense at last and sank back on the pillows.

The next few months were a very worrying time. Phyllis was frustrated and bored in bed, even though all her children took turns in visiting her. Caroline, in particular, spent a great deal of time with her, bringing little Anne along with her to amuse her as well. Tom marvelled at the difference in Caroline these days, and thanked his lucky stars that the last pregnancy had been straightforward, as they didn't have had much support back then. The only times when Phyllis did get up for 'calls of nature' etc., she started to feel immediately dizzy and ill. As the weeks went by, her hands and face did indeed swell up, and Tom was painfully reminded of Mary Ann's last days. He prayed with all his heart that his lovely Phyllis would get through this. He knew he couldn't bear to lose her.

As regards to the household, Tom engaged Bess again, from the village, to cook and clean. He tried his best to keep the garden going, working in the long summer evenings after he had finished a day's work at the yard. He found it quite therapeutic, however, as he had always liked growing things, and it helped to ease his mind. Nevertheless, he always made time to spend with Phyllis and little Joe. Joe was still a baby, but was beginning to toddle around now, which was difficult because Phyllis couldn't run around after him. Tom made him a playpen which they set up in the bedroom near Phyllis, so she could see and talk to him. When he needed feeding or changing, either Bess or Caroline brought him over to her in the bed, or if she was in pain, they did it for her. Tom also took his turn in the evenings and weekends. Phyllis suffered a great deal of abdominal pains and couldn't move far, even in bed.

Tom and Phyllis were no longer able to make love, but in bed at night Tom would hold her gently, caressing and talking to her, soothing away her frustrations and worries. She was sometimes irritable and often tearful, but Tom knew she couldn't help it. He tried his best to be patient as he knew it was not like her normally. After one particularly unhappy afternoon, Phyllis burst out crying, begging Tom for forgiveness.

"I'm so sorry!" she cried. "You don't deserve this. It's not your fault. I'm just so worried for the baby and I feel so ill. I'm sorry!"

"There's nothing to be sorry for," Tom reassured her. "I understand. You know I love you as much as ever and I just want you to be well." He kissed her and held her comfortingly. "It won't be much longer now."

On the whole, however, these incidents were rare and Phyllis did her best to bear it all with patience and fortitude. The doctor visited regularly, monitoring her and doing his best to treat her, but the condition persisted.

One day, towards the middle of September, the doctor told them that they really needed to consider inducing the birth early. The due date was the end of October, but Phyllis was so weak that the doctor was fearful for her.

"But what about the baby?" she asked. "I don't want to hurt it."

"It's only six weeks early," the doctor said. "It should be able to survive, and anyway you can't take the risk to your health much longer."

"Tom and I need to talk about it," said Phyllis. "I'm not sure. I can feel the baby kicking and I want to give it the best possible chance."

"Let me know tomorrow," Dr Smith said. "We can't wait too much longer. I'll need to make arrangements."

After he'd gone, Tom and Phyllis looked at each other in despair.

"I want to wait," she pleaded. "The baby needs more time. It's too early."

"Dearest Phyll," said Tom kindly. "You're risking your life. We already have one healthy child, who needs his mother. If we lose this one, then it's because it's the will of the Almighty. Hopefully we won't, but either way, we must look after you. We all need you."

After much heartfelt discussion they reached a compromise decision. They agreed the doctor could induce the birth 4 weeks before the due date, just to give another week or two for the baby. Tom prayed it wouldn't be too late for Phyllis, but the doctor agreed it seemed sensible and went ahead with the plans.

Therefore, on the 2nd of October, the doctor and midwife arrived and started the procedure. All Phyllis' children gathered anxiously to wait with Tom. They all knew it would be touch and go. Hours went by and Tom could hardly bear it. At one point, Fliss, the youngest daughter, held his hand whispering soothingly, "It'll be alright, Tom, honest. Mother's a fighter. She'll be okay."

Tom appreciated her kindness as he was almost at breaking point (Much later, he had cause to remember these words with sadness). The labour was long and difficult, but at last, at about six in the evening, Phyllis was delivered of a small but healthy baby girl. Tom rushed in as soon as he was allowed. Phyllis was very weak but miraculously okay. She just needed to rest and recover now. The doctor told them she would not be able to have any more children, but that he thought that this was for the best, considering her age and state of health this time. Tom knelt by her bed and held her close.

"Dearest Phyll," he murmured, "I love you and I'm so relieved you're alright. Just get well now."

Phyllis drifted off into a blissful state of unconsciousness, waking later feeling much refreshed and happy. She was desperate to see and hold her little girl.

"She's so beautiful, Tom, a little sister for Joe. Can we call her Ellen, please? I've always loved the name."

Tom's thoughts turned to an old lady who'd once helped him in his darkest hour, and replied he was only too happy, as it meant a lot to him.

It took a few days, but Phyllis and Ellen progressed well in spite of the difficult start. Tom felt relieved and happy, and couldn't wait to have his new family around him and to lead a normal life again. His hopes were answered only four weeks later, when Phyllis got out of bed and took up her usual domestic routine again, albeit with lighter duties. They could now get on with their lives and look to the future.

Chapter 28

Five years passed, which were good times for the family. The children both grew and thrived. Joe was an active boy who loved nothing more than to run and catch balls, whereas Ellen was quieter and loved animals of all kinds, particularly dogs. As she grew older, she kept pestering her parents to let her have one of her own, but they held out for the time being, saying she was too young. The two children were very different but loved each other dearly, though Joe would often tease Ellen about not being fast enough or agile enough to play ball with him. She, in turn, would fill his shoes with beetles or some other suitable creepy crawly, which would send him screaming from the room. Their parents loved them both and spent as much time as possible with them in the evenings and weekends, often picnicking down by the river or walking in the meadows.

They were also surrounded by an extended family of older children, brothers, sisters, cousins etc., as well as workers and friends. The tanning yard experienced a bit of a slow-down, but trade was still steady and there appeared to be no need for concern. The family even managed a trip to Devon one year, visiting all of Tom's siblings. They stayed with Lizzie and Daniel, who now had three grown up children of their own. Lizzie was the same caring person as ever and was much loved by everyone. Tom's older brother John had given up the fishmongers shop now and was working as a farm labourer. His wife had died a couple of years ago and his children had grown up and left home. Edward was happily married with several children who were all heading towards being gardeners. There was a developing trade in gardening and growing plants these days, so it seemed a good business to be in. Tom wished he had had the chance himself, but years ago there weren't the opportunities there were now. The youngest sister, Sarah, was a spinster who took in laundry and did some cleaning. She had once been engaged, but her fiancé died in the cholera outbreak of 1848 and she had never got over it. Tom enjoyed showing Phyllis all the places he had known as a child, and sharing his memories with her, both good and bad.

It was early in 1867, and Tom was surprised to learn that his son John was going to get married.

How did that happen? he thought. *How did I get old enough to have a son who is getting married and planning a family? It doesn't seem possible.*

But truth to tell, Tom was now over fifty years old and was beginning to feel it a bit. A few aches and pains had begun to trouble him of late and his eyesight for fine detail was not quite as good as it had been. When inspecting the quality of the finished leather now, he couldn't really see how good or bad it was. Still, it wasn't a worry at the moment. Everyone aged, he reasoned, if they didn't die first! He considered himself lucky; he knew first hand that life could be a struggle to survive.

In fact, Tom's son John wasn't the first one of their children to get married, as William had surprised him a couple of years earlier by coming to tell him that he was going to marry his childhood sweetheart and move to Bermondsey to work in the leather trade.

"But I thought you hated tanning," said Tom, confused.

"I do," sighed William. "But there's no work for me at the farm now and I need the money to be able to provide for my wife."

(The advent of cheap imported grain meant that farmers could not get much money for their corn any more, and what with the increasing mechanisation of farming, they didn't need so many workers, so William had been laid off).

"I have to give it a try," he said. "I appreciate what you did to help me get into farming, and I enjoyed it, but there's no future in it any more, unfortunately."

John Finnimore got married in St Mary's, Lambeth, near to where he'd been living and working of late. His bride was a local girl called Emma Errington. The family didn't meet her until just before the ceremony, but they took to her at once. She'd been working in Lambeth as a cap-maker, and was an industrious and lively young woman. She was always joking and laughing, which brought the more serious, quieter John out of himself.

John's sister, Molly, was also living in Lambeth now and was in service in a good household, acting as junior cook and kitchen maid. Although older than John, she had not yet found a young man to suit her, though there were many willing enough. She had the fine looks of her mother, but fortunately not the foolish temperament. However, John and Molly's early experiences had affected their self-confidence. They both found it hard to trust other people, in spite of their renewed relationship with their father and their acceptance of their mother's weakness of character. John had finally found someone to help heal him, but Molly was still searching. The siblings had become closer since Molly moved up to London, and consequently Molly was a witness at John's wedding. When Tom, Phyllis and their two children came up to London for the special occasion they were delighted to see John so happy at last, and also to have a chance to see Molly again. Tom had never forgotten his children from his first marriage, in spite of having a new life and family.

Tom had left their foreman, the ever-loyal Ed, in charge whilst they were away. He knew he was trustworthy and reliable. When they returned, however, they found Ed very anxious. The expected delivery of raw skins needed for their work as tanners had failed to turn up for the last two weeks. Unable to get in touch with anyone, Ed didn't know what to do for the best. The yard continued to work on the skins they already had, but there were currently no new ones. Tom sent an urgent message to their usual suppliers to see what was happening, but the reply dismayed him:

"Apologies, but all our raw skins are now being sent to Newcastle. Unfortunately, this means we will no longer be able to supply you with further items. Please accept our best wishes for the future."

Tom struggled to read all of this, but Bill, one of the younger men working in the yard, was able to clarify it for him. Tom went over immediately to talk to Phyllis about this. Having read the letter she then made some rapid enquiries via messenger to other local farmers and suppliers. Unfortunately, the reply was frequently the same – skins were being sent up north in bulk. Some smaller livestock farmers agreed to supply them with their raw materials, but the price was higher and the quantity limited. There was also the huge Rea and Fisher factory in Godalming, growing like a giant weed in a flowerbed, taking a great deal of the available trade. The trend was now increasingly towards factories rather than individuals. Industrialisation was taking its toll.

Later that same year, Phyllis' son Jack also announced he was getting married. He was rather young and so was his bride to be, but both sets of parents approved, so it went ahead. Shortly after they married, they followed William up to Bermondsey to live and work. With Fliss also working in service up in Mitcham, it seemed that everyone was moving away.

Time went by and the smaller local tanneries began to decline. They struggled on in Farncombe, but some of their men left to go and work at the big factory, and Tom didn't blame them. Unfortunately, lack of income meant that they couldn't afford to replace them. There just wasn't enough trade to justify it. This meant that the remaining men all had to take on more roles and work harder. Tom now had to do more manual work again, along with Ed and the rest, but he didn't complain. He desperately wanted to keep things going and hadn't realised how much he cared about it until now.

About halfway through 1868, however, the facts had to be faced. One evening, Tom, Phyllis and Ed sat down gloomily together to discuss the future.

"Well," said Phyllis. "I hate to say it, but we're only just about breaking even now, and we can't keep things going much longer."

"But we have to!" cried Tom. "For George's sake, if nothing else. He'd hate to see all his hard work come to nothing."

"Be realistic, Tom," Phyllis told him. "George has been dead ten years now and even he would have been able to see which way things are going. If we try and struggle on much longer, we'll end up in debt."

"I know," admitted Tom sadly. "But I feel bad about it. What about the men? They depend on the money." (He felt so guilty about this; he hated to hurt others)

Ed spoke up, "You're right there, Tom, but they can find other things. There's work at the factory or in other trades. You've both got to think of yourselves and your family."

"Oh Ed!" exclaimed Tom. "What will you do? I feel we've let you down."

"Hey, don't be daft!" said Ed. "I'm thinking of trying to take things easier soon anyway. It's all getting a bit much for me now." (Ed was already in his sixties and hadn't been that well recently.)

"I'm thinking of going back to a bit of farm work again. My neighbour was saying he could do with a hand."

So they reluctantly made the decision to wind up the business. After Ed had gone home, Tom and Phyllis sat down to discuss what they were going to do.

"I feel we need a new start somewhere different," Phyllis told him. "As you know, Fliss has been living and working up in Mitcham in Surrey, and she tells me that it's really nice. She says there's a new railway station just opened up which has made trade easier and that there still seems to be a lot of tanneries flourishing in the area. We'd be nearer all the family as well."

Tom could see the sense in this, but still felt like he was losing something precious. In spite of his original feelings about tanning he had enjoyed running a business and creating quality goods. He also knew he would miss Godalming where he had been so happy with Phyllis, but he knew the area was changing in character and that nothing remained the same forever. Maybe it *was* time for a change.

The last days of the yard were sad. Tom had to speak to the remaining employees and tell them the news. He apologised and gave them an extra payment to tide them over until they found new work. He was surprised to find himself welling up as he shook their hands and wished them all the best. On the final day with Ed all he could do was to hug him, speechless with emotion. Ed had helped him so many times and had been a true friend throughout. The usually jovial foreman tried to laugh it off, but it was a feeble attempt and Ed left the yard for the last time, wiping his eyes on the back of his sleeve.

Tom and Phyllis then set about winding up their affairs and planning their move to Mitcham. Fliss helped get a house for them to move into and she also made a few contacts with some local tanning yards for Tom to follow up when he got there. She was enthusiastic about their move and was looking forward to seeing more of her mother and stepfather. Ellen and Joe were also very excited, especially when they heard there was a large common land there and a cricket field in the town. They hoped to be able to play on the common and to enjoy the annual Mitcham fair. By all accounts the whole area smelled of lavender as this was a major local product. The very air was said to be sweetly perfumed. Maybe this was a good omen, thought Tom, as everyone knew that bad odours spread disease. It must be a healthy place to live.

Moving day came at last and the couple surveyed their almost empty house sadly. Boxes were packed and furniture was ready to be loaded. The carriers were coming at 10 o' clock that morning. There was nothing more to be got ready so they wandered aimlessly around the deserted rooms, remembering happier times. Ellen and Joe had a great time running around the house, shouting and chasing after each other, completely oblivious to their parents' distress. Tom put his arm around Phyllis' shoulders comfortingly.

"It'll be okay," he murmured, though he wasn't sure he really believed that.

After the final loading up, they left behind the empty shell of the house and went out into the yard. It was as silent as a tomb. Tom felt the wraith-like memories of past workers surround him, but knew it was time to move on. A developer had bought the yard and planned to build on it, and the house had been sold to another local family. Things change, he thought, then gathered up his family and left Farncombe behind forever.

Chapter 29

Mitcham was an interesting place, full of fields of fragrant lavender and other aromatic herbs at that time, as well as watercress beds by the river. The River Wandle flowed through it, but had been much altered by man to suit the needs of the area. There were many mills and industries along its banks, which provided a stark contrast to the more pastoral side of the town. Tanning was still a major industry here and Tom found it easy enough to get work, but it wasn't regular. He had to go back to being a journeyman again, working wherever and whenever anyone wanted him. Sometimes he was there for a few days, at other times a few months. Because he wasn't yet known in the area, he wasn't offered anything more permanent. There was also a big tanning factory in the town, but Tom resisted applying for work there. He hated the idea of working in a place like that. It was so big and soul-less. It would be almost like being back at Millbank again, imprisoned within walls of stone. At least when he worked outside, he felt free.

Because their income fluctuated, Phyllis started to take in washing in order to help out. Tom wished she didn't have to do this, but there was no option really. They had to pay the rent and feed the family. Fliss had found them a small terraced house in Beddington Corner, near the church, in a respectable working class neighbourhood, but it wasn't like having their own place. It was cosy enough however, and they soon settled in. Ellen and Joe started at the local school and found themselves welcomed by the other children. It seemed a friendly community. Their mother would often collect them from school and take them over to the Common to play for a while, which they enjoyed no end. Sometimes their school friends would join them.

In 1869, they heard the sad news that Caroline had been widowed, leaving her to cope with two young children. Tragically, her first child, Anne, who Tom had previously rescued from the river, had died from the dreaded diphtheria at the age of five. Thousands contracted this awful illness each year and it was usually fatal. Tom reflected that maybe poor little Anne had been fated from the start. It seemed that way for some people – life could be very cruel. The child mortality rate was currently very high, but the frequency of the deaths didn't make it any less heart-breaking for the parents.

There were two other children still for Caroline to take care of, but she was tough and practical, like her mother. So she packed up their expensive house in Westminster, which she knew she could no longer afford, and promptly moved to a cheaper area of London – Shoreditch. Here, she took work as a domestic servant whilst still managing to send her children to school. She was a proud woman who didn't let things get her down. The family offered her help, but she politely refused.

"I can manage," she said, and she did. She was a survivor.

Joe came running in to the kitchen one morning at breakfast time, saying, "Ma! Ellen won't get out of bed. She says she's poorly!"

Phyllis sighed. Ellen had had a bad cold for a few days now, sneezing and coughing a lot, but she really should be getting ready for school. Her mother marched into the bedroom, ready to do battle with a stubborn eight year old. What she saw there, however, frightened her.

"Come on, Ellen, it's time to get up," said Phyllis and drew the curtains.

Ellen groaned in pain at the light coming in and it was then that Phyllis noticed how swollen and watery her eyes were. She went closer and peered anxiously at her. The child's forehead was damp with sweat and when her mother put her hand on her brow, she could tell she was burning up with fever. Phyllis was suddenly very alarmed and drew back the sheets to see more. The whole of Ellen's chest and abdomen was covered in a pink rash.

"Don't worry, sweetie, stay in bed," she murmured. "Mummy will bring you something nice to eat."

Ellen just groaned again; the thought of food made her feel even worse.

When the doctor came, he pronounced that Ellen had measles, a potentially serious childhood illness which was also highly contagious. Many children were known to die from this disease and Phyllis felt very scared. However, the doctor reassured her that unless complications like pneumonia set in, with bed rest and good nursing care, Ellen should make a full recovery. However, having also examined Joe and found him to be free of any symptoms, he suggested that it might be a good idea for the boy to be kept well away, even out of the house if possible, to avoid being infected. After the doctor had gone therefore, Phyllis quickly arranged for Joe to go and stay with her youngest daughter for a while. As she also lived in Mitcham, he would still be able to attend school (although the doctor suggested he should be kept away from it for a few days as a precaution). Joe protested vigorously at this. He wanted to stay home and help look after Ellen, but his mother wouldn't hear of it.

"We can't have both of you ill, Joe," she said firmly. "It won't help Ellen, or any of us. I'm sorry but you have to go."

He was packed off on a cart to his older sister's house, but truth to tell, his eyes were full of tears as he left. He'd never been away from his home before and he suddenly felt very small, lonely and scared. In spite of his misgivings, nevertheless, Joe actually enjoyed himself over at his sister's. Fliss kindly took him over to the cricket field each day to watch the players and he became absolutely fascinated by the game, though of course, he still missed his family desperately.

When Tom came home from work in the evening, he was horrified to discover the situation. His wife was anxiously trying to nurse and feed Ellen in bed, his son was away and an air of panic existed in the house. Ellen was barely responsive, alternately shivering and burning with fever. Phyllis did her best to get fluids into her but it was difficult. When they finally went to bed that night, they both felt exhausted and worn out with worry.

The next couple of days were an anxious time. Tom had to go to work as otherwise they couldn't survive financially, but he spent the whole day thinking and worrying about Ellen. He felt powerless to help. Phyllis gave their daughter all the care and attention she possibly could, and eventually, both the rash and the fever seemed to be subsiding. The only remaining cause for concern was a nasty chesty cough which she didn't seem to be able to shake off. The cough racked Ellen's little body and left her exhausted and breathless. Still, she appeared to be getting better and was now sitting up in bed taking notice of things. Tom and Phyllis warily breathed a sigh of relief and hoped all would soon be well. The day after, however, Phyllis came into the bedroom in the morning to hear a dreadful rasping breath coming from her young daughter. Ellen was unconscious and could scarcely breathe. Phyllis ran over to fetch the doctor and to call Tom home from work. She knew this was serious now. The doctor confirmed it had turned to pneumonia and despite the treatment he prescribed for her, he estimated her chances only as fifty-fifty.

Tom and Phyllis were devastated. The doctor left and they collapsed in sorrow together. Their beautiful daughter! How could it be? It was so unfair! It brought back terrible memories for them both. Tom suddenly remembered dear little Annie dying of the cholera, and all the grief he'd been unable to express back then came back and overwhelmed him. Between sobs, he told Phyllis the story and she comforted him as best she could. Though she'd known he'd lost a sister, she'd never realised how traumatised he'd been by it until now. Then she related her own tragic loss of her son Henry, at the age of six, from scarlet fever. Tom had heard her talk of this before, but she had never gone into the details. Phyllis admitted to Tom now that this was one of the main reasons why George had shut himself off from her, despite her attempts at reconciliation. This is when all intimacy between them had ceased.

"I think he blamed me for not doing more," she told Tom. "But there was nothing else I could do. I'd just given birth to Jack as well and I didn't want him to catch it. It was an awful time."

Tom held her and soothed her distress. "You weren't to blame," he said. "There are so many dreadful diseases that can kill our children."

He broke down again, remembering the shameful scene at the churchyard.

"We couldn't even have a decent funeral for little Annie," he sobbed.

"Tom!" cried Phyllis suddenly. "Ellen's not baptised. If, (God preserve us) the worst happens, she can't have a Christian burial. What can we do?"

For some reason, they hadn't thought to get Ellen baptised earlier. It had just been forgotten in the everyday rush of living.

"I'll go and get the vicar!" exclaimed Tom. "I've heard that they'll come to the bedside when people are really ill. We need all the heavenly help we can get now."

He rushed off, glad to do something positive to help. He'd been feeling so useless the rest of the time.

So Ellen was baptised by the local vicar in her bed, unconscious, with her desperate parents looking on. The prayers that afternoon for her safe delivery from illness were the most heartfelt ones they'd ever said. Tom had always felt let down by the Almighty. After all, hadn't he let Annie die and sent Tom to prison, in spite of his prayers? Nonetheless, he begged Him with all his heart and soul to save his beloved daughter Ellen now.

Long, anxious hours went by with Ellen still struggling to breathe. As the first light of dawn came, however, and the sun started to rise, her breathing appeared to become easier and her cheeks lost the deathly pallor they'd had. They watched her, cautiously hoping for a miracle. It seemed the Almighty had indeed relented on this occasion and towards midday, Ellen sat up, rubbing her eyes and saying she was hungry. The worst was over and her parents could relax at last.

Ellen's progress back to full health was slow, nevertheless. She seemed to have no energy and little motivation to get out of bed. The doctor was pleased with her and advised her parents to get her up and about, but she tired easily and showed little interest in anything. Joe returned and this helped a bit, but whilst he was out at school she just sat in the chair in a stupor. All the activities her mother suggested were politely turned down. Phyllis was at her wit's end. One day, about two weeks after the crisis, Tom had an idea which he put to Phyllis. It was quite radical but she agreed it was worth a try. Consequently, when he came home the next day, he was carrying a small bundle of fluff, a scruffy looking mongrel puppy that he'd bought off a man in the street. He took him in to see Ellen and her eyes lit up for the first time since her illness.

"Pa – a dog! How wonderful. Is it for me?"

"Yes darling," he said. "He's all yours, but you've got to walk and feed him properly. He's called Sharp, just like the Queen's collie dog."

Ellen flung herself at her father and hugged him so hard she nearly strangled him, then she gathered up the puppy and smothered it with kisses. The puppy loved her at first sight and became her loyal companion and friend. No longer was Ellen the gloomy invalid, she was back to her normal, enthusiastic self.

Chapter 30

1871 was a year of wedding celebrations. Tom's daughter, Molly, finally met someone who captured her heart. A handsome young gardener working at the same grand house where Molly was assistant cook caught her eye. He very soon noticed the beautiful, quiet young woman who worked so hard in the kitchen and was keen to make her acquaintance. James Cooper, for that was his name, found every excuse to come into the house. He brought fresh vegetables for the table and flowers for the vases, and then he started bringing flowers for her. Molly blushed, accepted them shyly and a relationship developed. Jim was a kind, honest, hardworking man, and when Molly finally took him to meet her father, Tom took to him immediately. They were married in Lambeth on 8th May 1871 and made their home nearby. Everyone was very happy for them.

Just before this, however, another wedding had taken place which both Tom and Phyllis had some misgivings about. Phyllis' youngest daughter, Fliss, met a young man called Henry Keen, who swept her off her feet in a matter of weeks. Theirs was an intense, passionate relationship and it was clear that Henry adored Fliss. Nevertheless, there was something about him that they couldn't quite take to. Henry was a darkly brooding type of man, with a shock of black hair and a forbidding looking beard. As soon as he started courting Fliss they saw less and less of her. The couple quickly announced their engagement and planned their wedding for April 22nd at Mitcham. Henry appeared to be taking over her life, and Tom commented to Phyllis that he didn't think Fliss was her usual self these days.

"She's different," he said. "More distant. I think we're losing her."

"I know what you mean," agreed Phyllis. "But it's her life and we mustn't interfere."

It was early April and Tom had to go down to Shalford to work for a week in order to make enough money to help pay for the weddings. He hated being away from home, but he *was* looking forward to being back around Godalming again. He was going to be lodging with Ed and his family, so it would be a great chance to catch up. As Tom was going to be away, Phyllis was therefore able to persuade Fliss (and more to the point, her fiancé Henry) that she needed help and company for the week.

"It'll be great to spend some time together," she said, "before you finally become a married lady."

Henry wasn't very pleased about it, but Fliss agreed and he couldn't stop her.

Tom went off to Shalford therefore, happy in the knowledge that the two women would have some space to themselves. Ed was the same as ever, teasing Tom for all he was worth. Tom realised he'd missed him and vowed to visit again before too long.

Mother and daughter had an enjoyable week together but at the end of it, Phyllis realised that Fliss had never actually said that she loved Henry. She felt worried that her daughter might be missing out on something special, and although she hoped she was wrong, she feared the worst.

The wedding took place on a lovely spring morning and all appeared to go well. After the ceremony, Fliss came up and hugged her mother, whispering in her ear, "Thank you for everything you've done for me, Mother."

Phyllis just hugged her back, saying, "You know I'll always be here for you darling, if you need me."

However, after the couple had settled down in their new home, none of the family saw much of her any more. They heard from mutual friends that Fliss rarely left the house and had become very much under Henry's control.

Later that same year, they also attended a more understated wedding when Caroline got married to George Summers, an older man who was happy to take on the two children and give them all a home. During the wedding breakfast, Caroline came up to Phyllis and Tom smiling, and said, "You know what, Mother? I've just done exactly what I blamed you for all those years ago. I'm sorry. You were quite right – everyone deserves a second chance at happiness."

She turned to Tom. "I was so wrong about you, Tom. You're a good man who's made Mother very happy."

Tom smiled and hugged her. "That's all in the past," he told her. "No need to worry about it now."

In April 1872, Tom and Phyllis were summoned to Fliss' bedside where she was about to give birth to her first child. They'd hardly seen her lately, but Fliss was desperate to have her mother with her for the birth so Henry relented and sent for them. Tom spent much time talking to Henry whilst they waited anxiously for the new arrival. He hoped maybe he could get to understand this deep and mysterious man and tried to chat gaily about babies and families, but Henry sat there morosely brooding, barely responding. Tom understood his fears – childbirth was a dangerous business – and put it down to that. He remembered Fliss' kindness to him when Phyllis had been giving birth to Ellen, and hoped she would be okay.

Phyllis spent her time in with the midwife, trying to comfort Fliss, but it was a very difficult labour. As the baby finally arrived, Fliss was torn and damaged, and despite everything the midwife could do, she was haemorrhaging badly. Phyllis rushed out to the two men.

"Please. Fetch the doctor!" she cried. "Fliss needs help at once!"

Tom looked at Henry – did he want to go, or should he? He waited a moment in an agony of indecision, then asked him, "What do you want me to do?"

"Go, man!" shouted Henry. "Please! I must be with my wife."

Tom dashed off and Henry went in to see Fliss, despite the midwife's protests. The new-born baby was screaming healthily, but Fliss lay there bleeding to death. Henry knelt by her bedside, tears pouring down his face, and Phyllis stood nearby, helplessly.

A few minutes later, Tom reappeared with the doctor, who did what he could. It was all too late however, too much blood had been lost and Fliss went into a downward spiral. In her last few minutes, she called for her mother.

"Ma," she whispered weakly. "Look after my baby for me. He's called Henry after his father."

"I'll look after him till you're better," Phyllis promised her, knowing that this would probably never happen, but trying to give her hope. "You'll soon be up and around again."

The words were hollow and Phyllis knew it. She moved aside to let Henry say his last goodbyes, then Tom put his arm around her shoulder and led her weeping from the room. Moments later, Fliss was gone.

The day before Fliss' funeral, Phyllis and Tom sat down to discuss what needed to be done for the baby. Immediately after Fliss' death, Henry had declared that he never wanted to see it again.

"Take it away!" he demanded of them. "If you don't I may do something rash. It killed my wife."

They sorrowfully collected the tiny bawling infant and took them back to their house. Phyllis was devastated by her daughter's death, but having the baby to think about helped her get through this awful time. Tom gave her all the support he could, as always.

Phyllis was hopeful that with time Henry might be reconciled with his son, but Tom was more realistic.

"You know," he told Phyllis, "even if Henry decides he wants the child, how *can* he look after it? He has to work. I know from my own experience that a working man can't look after young children on his own. That's why I had to let Mary Ann take Molly and John away."

"I know, Tom," Phyllis agreed. "But that means someone in the family will need to take it in, unless he gets a nanny, and I don't think he can afford that. Will and Jack are up to their ears in young children already and Caroline is pregnant now, so who can help?"

Tom looked at her. "Well," he said hesitantly, "it's probably a foolish idea, but there's always us."

She stared at him in disbelief. "You mean you'd be prepared to take on another baby?" she asked.

"Well yes," he replied. "But it would be you who it falls on mostly, so you need to think about whether *you* could cope."

"Ellen and Joe are older now," Phyllis said thoughtfully, "and they could help out as well. You're right – we are the only ones who don't have very young children already, and I did promise poor dear Fliss that I'd look after him for her. Tom, you're a wonderful man to think of it. I love you!"

"Let's see what the others think tomorrow," said Tom cautiously. "And what his father wants to do. Maybe he would want to keep him, if we were able to baby-sit while he was working. It's up to him at the end of the day."

After the funeral service, they all gathered back at Henry's house to pay their respects. When he saw Phyllis come in, carrying his son, however, he cried, "Take that murdering monster away! I never want to see it again."

"He's your son, Henry," reasoned Phyllis gently. "It's not his fault. Look at him. Here, hold him for a while."

She tried to give the baby to his father but he pushed her away angrily. "Never!" he exclaimed.

"Take him to the Foundling's Hospital. It's all he deserves!"

"Look, let's talk through this as a family," suggested Tom and got everyone to sit down. "Does anyone feel able to take him into their home?"

"We can't," said Jack. "Not with just having had a new baby ourselves. We're sorry. My wife feels really bad about it."

"I talked to my missus yesterday," said Will. "But she's not been at all well herself lately and we just can't. It'd be too much for her."

Caroline sighed. "I don't think George would like it," she said. "Not with our first child on the way in a few months."

Tom looked at Phyllis and nodded silently to her.

She then spoke up, "Would anyone object if we took him on? Henry – do you mind? You'd be welcome to visit him any time, and if you feel able to give him a home later, then that would be fine as well. He's still your son."

"Take him!" he said. "I've told you. I don't want him. Now if you don't mind, can you all please go and leave me in peace!"

They were shocked at his rudeness and his hard-hearted attitude, but retreated to the comfort of Tom and Phyllis' house to mourn their loss and repair hurt feelings. Here they were able to properly pay tribute to their dear Fliss and to grieve in peace.

"I shall call him Harry, not Henry," Phyllis told Tom later that evening, when everyone had gone home. "For one thing, I've already lost one child called Henry so it might be bad luck to use the name again, and for another thing, I certainly don't want to call him after his father!"

Chapter 31

Little Harry had just turned five when Tom made the decision to give up tanning. The year before, Tom had turned sixty and had decided that being a journeyman tanner was no longer for him. All that travelling and working in different places was getting too hard now. Work was scarcer and he was being asked to spend more time away from home, which he hated. So he finally relented and went to work in the big factory, Wandle Tannery. However, he immediately regretted his decision. The factory employed over a hundred men and boys, and the noise of people and machinery was deafening. Tom found it claustrophobic and oppressive. The steam and fumes bellowed out as if from an angry dragon, polluting the atmosphere and making it hard to breathe. It was rumoured that several men had left recently with chest problems. Tom had never liked crowds in confined spaces anyway, since his time in prison, and so found the constant pressure of people almost unbearable, but he struggled to cope and the months went by.

Not only that, but the tannery used the newer, faster, chromium based method of tanning, which was a lot more toxic. He saw men with terrible skin rashes who still managed to keep working in spite of it all. Chromium had started being used in the late 1850s, but Phyllis' yard had stuck to the traditional method of vegetable tannin, which was just as effective but slower. Once Tom started working for other yards, he came across the increased use of chromium, but he treated it with the utmost caution. It was a dangerous and unpleasant substance, which also polluted the local rivers with its waste products.

Children had always had to start work at an early age to help support their families. Tom himself had been working from the age of 12 and his own children had not been much different. However, consideration had been given to their age, and the duties adjusted accordingly. No such thought was given to the factory boys, however. They worked 10-hour days with the rest of them and were often tasked with the most dangerous jobs of cleaning around and underneath moving machinery. Only last week, Tom had heard the gruesome story of a ten-year-old boy being killed by being caught up in one of the machines.

The overseer was a brutal man who was quick to punish anyone, man or boy, found slacking. Tom had seen him give boys a beating before, although only from a distance. He hated to think that any child of his should ever end up in a place like this. One day, Tom walked into a section just as a boy came running in late from break. The overseer caught him and berated him loudly.

"Where've you been, you little devil?" he shouted, cuffing him 'round the 'ear.

"Sorry, Mister!" the boy cried. "I fell asleep, sir."

But this was the wrong thing to say. It was like a red rag to a bull. The overseer pulled the boy along by his ear to an area where wood was stored. He flung him down on the floor and picked up a stout stick.

"Fall asleep, would yer? You lazy little good fer nuthin – I'll learn yer!"

He swung the stick, but Tom could take no more and leapt forward with a cry of, "No! Leave him alone!"

He never stopped to think of the consequences of his actions, but he couldn't stand by and watch this. The overseer was furious. He pulled the boy to his feet and threw him at Tom.

"Oh, so you know best do yer? Two of a kind, I s'pose! Clear out, the pair of you. You're both fired. Now get lost or I'll set the coppers on yer! We don't want folks like you 'round 'ere."

Police! This was a terrifying thought. Tom rapidly collected his things and walked out, the boy by his side, but instead of gratitude for his rescue the boy was angry and bitter.

"Now look what you done, Mister! Thanks a bloomin' lot. Now I've done lost me job and me Ma's going to be proper cross with me."

Tom stared at him, not knowing what to say. "I thought I was helping," he muttered.

"Well you weren't!" retorted the boy. "Go help someone else next time."

Then he ran off in the opposite direction. Tom sighed. Now what was he going to do? How could he tell Phyllis he'd lost his job? He'd lasted barely a year there and knew he couldn't go back to tanning. It was over for him now.

Phyllis was surprised and worried to see Tom arrive home from work so early.

"Tom, what's wrong?" she asked. "Are you ill? You don't look well."

Tom wasn't ill but was feeling desperate. Without a word, he came in and sat down heavily on a chair, his head in his hands.

"Tom, darling. What is it?" Phyllis asked again. "Whatever it is, you can tell me. We'll work it out."

"I'm so sorry," he mumbled. "I've lost my job! I've let you down, I know, but I can't take any more."

Phyllis just held him close, murmuring words of comfort to him, until he felt able to tell her the whole story. She listened carefully and reassured him that there was no shame in how he'd behaved.

"I'm proud of you for standing up for the boy," she told him. "Even if he didn't appreciate it. That man could have killed him."

"I can't go back to tanning anymore," said Tom. "I just can't do it. I'm sorry!"

When all the family came home at the end of the day, Phyllis asked them all to come in and sit down. Joe and Ellen were both working now; Joe as a labourer and Ellen doing sewing and mending for some local ladies. Harry, of course, was in bed by the time they came in.

"Your father and I have had a long talk today," Phyllis began.

"That sounds serious!" said Ellen, alarmed.

"It's nothing to worry about," her mother reassured her, smiling. "It's just that we think it's time for a change. Your father has decided to leave tanning and do something different, and we were wondering if it might be a good idea to move."

"Move where?" asked Joe.

"Well, that's what we want to talk to you about," Tom said. "We'd like to hear your opinions as well. Of course, you're both old enough now to leave home and make your own way, if you want to, but we'd still like to have your views. There are two options really – either we could move into London, nearer the rest of the family, or we could move out into the countryside again."

"Well, to be absolutely honest," said Joe. "I was going to talk to you about it, but I really want to train as a chemist and there's nowhere 'round here that will take me on. If we were in London I'd have a lot more chances. Caroline was only saying the other day that she thought she could introduce me to someone near her."

"In Shoreditch?" Phyllis queried. "Well, that was one place we were considering."

"I've heard it's very rough, though," Ellen said, frowning. "I *do* want to move into London as well, but I've heard there are slums 'round there."

"That's true," agreed her mother. "But St Leonards, where Caroline lives, is the nicest part, and it is cheap there. We'd be close to her and near the rest of the family as well."

"I am a bit worried, though," said Tom. "What sort of work can I get now? I'm too old to start learning a new trade, and I need something lighter. My back's not very good these days."

"There must be lots of opportunities in London, Father," said Ellen. "I'm sure you'd find something. I'd really like to get into service in a big house as a ladies maid. There's very little in the way of grand houses here anymore, so I'd rather move into the city."

It was true. Mitcham was rapidly losing its village atmosphere. The lavender fields were fast disappearing as more and more industry grew daily, like a virus. The air didn't smell of herbs any more, but of soot and grime.

"What about Harry?" asked Joe.

"He's too young to worry about where he lives," replied Phyllis. "He'll come with us."

"Oh I know that," said Joe. "But I just wondered about his father. He won't know where to find him anymore."

"Look Joe," his mother said. "His father has made no contact with him in five years, and by all accounts, has moved away, so I don't think he will care, quite honestly."

Shoreditch was certainly a lively place, full of opportunities. The whole area had a vibrancy to it that was almost palpable. The place was buzzing with music hall and theatres by night, and small traders and artisans peddling their wares by day. There were masses of furniture and craft shops, along with just about every other business you could think of. True, it did indeed have a notorious slum called the Old Nicholl, but they were well away from that. They rented a small terraced house near Caroline and her family, and soon settled in.

Caroline was good to her word and managed to get Joe in on the bottom rung of a chemists business, just as a packer to start with, but with opportunities to progress. He worked hard, but nevertheless still found time to join the local cricket club.

Tom was unsure what to do at first, but a chance meeting with a local shopkeeper gave him an idea. He'd gone into a local grocery shop to enquire whether they needed any help, but the man replied he was sorry but no, he wasn't hiring. Just as Tom was about to leave, another man came rushing out of the back of the shop saying, "'Ere George, you need to get a message to the market to let 'em know we need more supplies of spuds."

"I can't leave the shop," George said. "Can't you go?"

"I gotta unload these 'ere apples," the man replied.

George turned to Tom. "'ere mate," he said. "If you want to earn a couple of bob, go to the market, see Len on the veg stall and ask him to send ten sacks of spuds double quick. Come back 'ere with his reply and I'll pay yer, okay?"

So Tom did it gladly, keen to do something positive and earn some money. When he had returned and been paid, the shopkeeper said, "You could always do that for a living, mate. I've heard there's lots of call for reliable messengers, 'specially in the city. It's not bad income either, though you're always on yer feet."

So Tom became a licensed messenger, taking important documents between businesses in the city. He enjoyed the work because it was varied, interesting and he was out of doors around London most of the time. He got to know the streets of the city very well, and there weren't many places he couldn't find. He also enjoyed talking to all the different people he met in his travels.

Meanwhile, Ellen took work in a fashionable doctor's house in Finsbury Square. Because it was so close to where they lived, she was still able to live at home, which pleased her greatly as she couldn't bear the thought of leaving her dog, Sharp. Though she worked long hours as a parlour maid, she still found time to take him for regular walks. He was her faithful friend and would sit in the front room, watching for Ellen to come home each night.

Most of their family lived nearby, either in Shoreditch, or south of the river in Lambeth or Bermondsey. The only one who didn't was Phyllis' oldest son, William, who had finally seen sense, given up the tanning again and moved back to Godalming to work in a paper mill.

"You were right," he told Tom. "I was stupid to think I could last in this job, especially with the way the industry's changed. This London air's not doing my wife's health any good, either. I think we'll do better back in the country again."

Early in 1881 they mourned the sad loss of Sharp, at the age of eleven, a pretty good age for any dog in those days. He had slowed down a lot in the last year and eventually slipped away peacefully in his sleep. Ellen was heartbroken and said home didn't feel the same any more. It felt so empty. Coming back in the evening, without him waiting to greet her, was almost unbearable. She was now nearly 19 years old and decided it was time to move out. She found herself a good job as a ladies maid in a house in Ecceleston Square, Belgravia, to two elderly sisters. She was delighted to find that the younger sister, a wheelchair bound widow, had a small lapdog which required grooming, feeding and walking. Ellen was only too happy to include these extra chores in her duties, even though Lulu Belle was a temperamental and spoilt Pomeranian.

Having become a regular player in the local cricket team, Joe also got friendly with the other players, in particular an older man called Walter Wiseman, who invited him back for some post-match refreshments one afternoon. It was there that Joe met and fell in love with Walter's daughter, Susannah, and they were very soon courting.

As Harry got older, he kept asking them where his parents were. He knew he lived with his grandparents and that his mother was dead, but they kept sparing him the details. Phyllis said to Tom that she didn't feel the child should grow up with a burden of guilt on his shoulders and Tom agreed, but felt that sooner or later, Harry would need to know the truth. The child admired Tom greatly and loved to go walking around London with him on a Saturday morning whilst Tom was working. Tom was 65 now and had to take things slower. Harry would often rush up the steps to collect things for him.

"I want to be a messenger like you, Grandpa!" he declared, and later on that's exactly what he would become.

One Saturday, however, Harry was very quiet and thoughtful as they progressed on their way. He was now ten years old and just about to finish school. Tom sensed something was wrong, but let the boy come to it in his own time.

"Grandpa," said Harry suddenly. "Why doesn't my Pa live with us? My friends say their Ma and Pa are helping them find jobs. Where is he? Doesn't he care about me? What happened to Mama?"

"That's a lot of questions!" said Tom. "But I think it's time you knew. Your poor dear Mama died giving birth to you. It wasn't your fault. The midwife wasn't very good and your Ma was never very strong."

"What was she like?" asked Harry.

"She was a gentle person, very kind and thoughtful, and she loved you dearly in the little time she had. She asked your Grandma to look after you for her," replied Tom. "We always called her Fliss, but her name was Phyllis really, the same as your Granny. She had light brown hair, just like yours. You look a lot like her, actually."

"Where's my father?" Harry asked again. "Is he dead too?"

"No," said Tom hesitantly. "But he couldn't take care of you because he was working, so we offered to take you."

"But why doesn't he come to see me?" Harry persisted. "He's my father!"

"I'm sorry to say," explained Tom, as kindly as he could, "that he was so upset when your mother died, that he felt he couldn't face seeing you. I'm afraid he blamed you for her death. I'm sorry but that's the truth, and we've tried to keep it from you because we think he's being unfair. He's a moody and difficult man and you're better off without him."

Harry paused to take it all in. "So he hates me then?" he said.

"Well, that's maybe too strong a word," Tom replied. "But he said he didn't want to see you again. I'm sorry Harry. You know *we* love you."

They continued their walk in silence for some time, then Harry suddenly burst out, "Well I don't want to see him, either!

Grandpa, you and Grandma are *my* family and I love you all for it. *You're* all I need and I'll always be grateful to you."

"Harry dear, you don't need to feel grateful," Tom reassured him. "You're part of our family and that's all there is to it."

Harry never spoke of his father again, realising that the people who *really* want you are the most important, no matter what relationship they are to you.

Chapter 32

In 1833 Joe married Susannah Wiseman in St James' Church, Shoreditch, with the whole family there to celebrate. The couple didn't waste any time in starting to produce children of their own. Tom and Phyllis were now both well into their late sixties and were having to slow down. They only worked part time now, but still got by financially because all the family helped out with money whenever they could. They were beginning to enjoy a semi-retirement and were able to spend more time together, dozing by the fire or relaxing in their tiny garden. Tom finally got to do some gardening which made him happy, although he had to be careful not to overdo it. Phyllis took to embroidery, even though her eyesight was not as good as it had been. Happily, Harry was able to take over many of Tom's messenger duties. Things seemed to have settled down at last.

Ellen was still working at the house in Belgravia and mostly enjoying it. Admittedly, the older sister, Miss Rowland, could be demanding at times, and Emma, the cook, could be very bossy; but Mrs Gray, the younger sister, was kind and often gave Ellen the chance to get out and about on errands for her. One afternoon, Ellen took Lulu Belle to the park for her usual walk. It was a sunny day with a strong breeze and a feeling of spring in the air. Lulu Belle was very frisky on this particular day, darting here and there as Ellen tried to walk her down by the little stream. Ellen had been here a few times recently and on several occasions had said good afternoon to a handsome young policeman patrolling the park. He had a nice smile, she thought, but wondered why it was that she ran into him so often.

Suddenly, Lulu Belle saw a duck landing on the water and took off after it, more like a retriever than a tiny pampered Pomeranian. The lead snapped and Ellen suddenly realised that Lulu Belle was free and no longer under her control. She tried to grab her, but the little dog was in no mood to be caught. She raced off across the park, yapping furiously at all the birds. Ellen gathered up her long skirts as best she could and ran after her, calling frantically, but it was a fruitless chase. Half an hour later, Lulu Belle was nowhere to be seen and Ellen was in a state of despair. She collapsed onto one of the park benches, out of breath and in tears. Her Mistress loved that dog and would be very upset if she was lost. Not only that, but Ellen would be fired without a doubt. As she sat there crying, she gradually became aware of someone approaching. It was the young policeman she always said hello to.

"Are you alright, miss?" he asked. "Can I help in any way?"

She blurted out the details. "It's my Mistress's dog! She's run away, and I can't find her, and I'm going to be in awful trouble."

"Come on," he said kindly. "I'll help you look. I'm sure we'll find her."

It took them some time walking the whole of the park, the policeman questioning people they met, before someone said they'd seen her annoying the ducks, down by the pond on the other side of the park. As they went, the policeman told her something about himself.

"I'm PC Alderman," he said. "But my first name's John. My family comes from Cambridgeshire but I always wanted to join the London police force so I moved here."

Ellen also told him about herself and her family.

"I used to have my own dog, Sharp," she said. "But he died a couple of years ago and I miss him so much." The tears flowed again. "He was a much more sensible dog than this one."

Eventually, Lulu Belle was retrieved by PC Alderman, who then created a makeshift lead and helped Ellen get the unrepentant dog home. Lulu Belle seemed none the worse for her adventure, but Ellen's nerves were in shreds. She couldn't thank the policeman enough for his help. She was late home, but made an excuse that she'd been talking to some other dog owners in the park and forgotten the time, so her Mistress never knew about Lulu Belle's escapade.

On one of her visits home on a Sunday, Ellen told her parents all about a nice young man she'd met, who she wanted to invite home for tea.

"You'll like him," she said enthusiastically. "He's very respectable."

She'd been meeting John regularly ever since the incident and they had become very close. Out of uniform, she could see that he was tall, with fine sandy coloured hair and twinkling blue eyes. He had a kind manner and an infectious laugh.

"We'd love to meet him, darling," said Phyllis. "Why not bring him 'round next week?"

The following week, they were waiting expectantly for Ellen's young man to appear when there was a knock at the door. Tom went to answer it and was shocked by what he saw. It was a policeman in uniform on the doorstep! Tom turned pale with fear.

"Can I help you?" he asked nervously, hoping the man hadn't come to take him away for some reason.

"I'm sorry I've come in uniform," the man said. "But I have to go back on duty again in a couple of hours, so it was easier to come as I am."

"Sorry?" said Tom, thoroughly confused.

Just then Ellen came rushing to the door.

"John!" she exclaimed. "Come in. father, don't keep him standing on the doorstep."

She led him past a stunned Tom into the living room. Phyllis also looked surprised and concerned.

"Is everything alright?" she asked.

"This is John Alderman, Mother," Ellen said.

"You never told us what he did," pointed out Phyllis. "I'm sorry, Mr Alderman, we weren't expecting a policeman. I thought something awful had happened."

After the initial surprise, the meeting went well, but Tom was very quiet throughout. He was still terrified of the law and it brought back bad memories. Phyllis did her best to keep the conversation going and it was obvious that John was a cheerful, easy-going man who was genuinely fond of their daughter. He also talked briefly of his love of policing.

"There are so many criminals around these days," he said. "If I can make any difference then I'll do my best to try. This world needs cleaning up, so that decent folks like you can enjoy their lives in peace."

After John and Ellen had left, Tom looked at Phyllis. "How did that happen?" he said. "A daughter of mine, courting a copper! If he finds out about my past he'll be gone like a shot."

"Come off it, Tom," said Phyllis. "It was over forty years ago now! We *are* decent folks, like he said. You've nothing to be ashamed of."

"But what if *he* doesn't agree?" asked Tom. "You heard what he said about cleaning up the world."

"You've served your time, Tom," she reassured him. "What's done is done. Forget it!"

But Tom had bad dreams that night, where people were gathering to take him away to prison, and no matter what he said, no one would listen to him. He woke up in a cold sweat. He'd not consciously thought about prison in years, but it was always there in the back of his mind, a dark shadow in his past. He realised suddenly that neither Ellen nor Joe knew anything about it. It had happened so long before they were born that he'd just never got 'round to telling them. He hadn't deliberately hidden it. They knew all about their previous marriages and children of course, but not further back. Like all children, they hadn't thought to ask, and their parents hadn't thought to tell them. It just didn't seem relevant any more.

However, it soon became relevant when John turned up a few weeks later to ask for Ellen's hand in marriage. Ellen was with him, flitting about excitedly, a mixture of joy and nervousness on her face. She left the room with Phyllis, ostensibly to make the tea, and Tom knew the moment had come. In the last few weeks, he'd been plagued by bad dreams, where he was shut in a darkened cell again or back on the hulks, but he'd vowed to try and forget it all for Ellen's sake. If he never told them, then it wouldn't be a problem, he reasoned. Why should they need to know anyway?

John Alderman sat down awkwardly.

"Sir," he said nervously. "I think you know why I'm here. I love your daughter Ellen and I would like to make her my wife, with your permission and blessing, I hope."

He paused anxiously, looking at Tom. Tom swallowed hard.

"Of course," he said, trying to sound pleased about it. "I know you'll make her very happy. Will you stay in the police force?"

189

"Oh yes!" said John enthusiastically. "It's my life and it's a good career. I can afford to look after Ellen well; you don't need to worry about her."

"I'm sure," said Tom, trying to come to terms with it all. "Now let's get the ladies back in and celebrate!"

All went well until John mentioned something which shattered Tom's confidence.

"Of course there is a vetting procedure for police constables when they get married," he explained. "But it's nothing to worry about. It's just a formality."

"What's that?" Tom asked anxiously.

"Well, being in the police our liaisons have to be checked for criminal connections. Obviously, a policeman could be influenced or coerced if they had relatives with a criminal background. So they do a check to make sure this doesn't happen." He laughed. "There won't be any problem with you folks anyway, will there?"

"What do we have to do?" asked Phyllis, concerned.

"Oh there's a few forms to fill in. I'll bring them over next week. Then the Inspector just clears everything and gives his permission. It doesn't take long."

Tom had turned as white as a sheet. "Forms?" he said. "How far back do they look?"

"Oh they go right back," replied John. "But it's nothing to worry about."

Tom and Phyllis both spent many sleepless nights worrying about the vetting procedure. Tom hated to think his past might spoil Ellen's happiness. Phyllis tried hard to reassure him that it would be okay, but she wasn't totally convinced herself.

"We should tell them both," she said. "They've got to know sooner or later."

"I'll talk to them next week," agreed Tom. "When they bring the forms over." He dreaded the thought of it.

John and Ellen came over the following Sunday afternoon, both very happy and confident when they arrived.

Phyllis started to read the top of the forms... "Where the relatives of a constable are found to have spent or unspent convictions for recordable offences, the following will be considered: the likelihood that the constable's performance of duty will be adversely affected through adverse pressure or a conflict of interests…." There was more, but Phyllis hesitated to read further.

"It seems very serious," she said.

"Sit down, both of you," said Tom. "We need to talk. I have something to tell you."

They looked a bit surprised, but did as they were told. There was a pause whilst Tom tried to summon up the courage.

"There's a problem," he began, hanging his head in shame. "The fact is, I do have a criminal conviction from years ago."

"Father!" exclaimed Ellen. "What do you mean? How come you never said anything?"

Tom sighed. "I never thought I would need to," he said.

John looked concerned. "Tell me all about it, sir," he said calmly. "Then we'll see what can be done." He didn't seem unduly worried.

"It was a very long time ago," said Phyllis pleadingly. "Maybe it won't matter."

"So you knew as well, Mother!" Ellen cried.

"I'm afraid so," she murmured. "I'm sorry."

Tom told John and Ellen all the details of his crime, his trial and his time in prison and they listened in stunned silence. However, he also mentioned his pardon, which John seemed to think might make a difference.

"I'll look into it. Try not to worry," he told them all.

John left the forms with them and went back to his duties, leaving Ellen with them. She was furious and turned on her father angrily.

"How could you do this to me, Father? Why didn't you tell me? You're ruining my happiness. If I can't marry John I'll never speak to you again!"

"Please, Ellen," begged Tom. "Don't be like that! I didn't mean to hurt you. It was a foolish mistake made years ago, which I've paid for dearly. It keeps coming back to haunt me again and again, first with your mother and now with you. I'm so sorry. If I could have my time over again I'd have never have been that stupid, but I can't. I'm sorry!"

But nothing he could say would calm Ellen down and she left that afternoon, barely talking to either of them.

At her brother, Joe's house the next day, Ellen was still in a state of distress.

"Why didn't we know about it?" she stormed. "Why did he hide it?"

"Perhaps he was ashamed or embarrassed," said Joe calmly.

"Did *you* know about it?" she demanded.

"No, not really," he replied. "But I knew there was something odd about my birth. I did the maths and it turns out that Mum and Dad weren't married when they had me. Caroline told me there was a problem, so they couldn't get married any earlier. The family disapproved of Dad apparently. She said she felt a bit guilty about it, but wouldn't tell me why. Maybe this explains it."

"Oh Joe," said Ellen tearfully. "What am I going to do? I love John and I want to marry him!"

"Would it have made any difference if you knew about Dad earlier?" asked Joe. "It wouldn't have stopped you loving John, would it? If John really loves you, he'll marry you anyway. You need to forgive Dad. It's not really his fault."

"Maybe not," admitted Ellen. "But I can't forgive him at the moment."

Chapter 33

John Alderman came back for the forms the following week. Phyllis had spent all week trying to fill them in for Tom. They asked so much – dates, times, details of conviction, punishment, release, employment, character references, etc. Tom struggled to remember all the precise details now, it was so long ago. They gave Ed Johnson, their ex-foreman, as a character reference. He was in his seventies now, but had known and worked with Tom for over ten years. Between them they managed to complete the forms, but they were both tired and stressed. They'd hardly slept all week.

"Is there any documentation?" asked John Alderman. "Proof of your pardon or anything else? It would really help, you know."

"I have a letter," said Tom. "But it's all I have and I don't want to lose it."

"I promise I'll look after it," John reassured him (and he proved to be as good as his word).

Tom reluctantly fetched it out of the old wooden box that Phyllis had given him as a Christmas present when they first knew each other. He still kept his most precious belongings in it. The letter was faded and brown with age, but luckily was still readable. It clearly stated his pardon and was dated 1837.

"I'm sure this will make a big difference," John told him. "Look, Mr Finnimore, please don't worry about it all. I respect you for your courage in telling us this."

"Ellen doesn't see it that way," Tom mumbled.

"She will," said John. "I've already told her that I'll marry her anyway, even if I have to leave the police force. She's far more important to me than that."

"Really?" Tom said, surprised. "I thought the police force was your life."

"It was," replied John. "But that was before I met Ellen."

When John left he shook Tom's hand warmly. They'd talked all afternoon and reached a new understanding. Tom no longer felt scared of him and, for the first time all week, slept through the night without any bad dreams.

Weeks went by, however, and in spite of the fact that John had indeed talked to Ellen, she didn't re-appear at their house. The vetting process dragged on slowly. More details were required at intervals and they had become heartily sick of it all. Joe visited to tell them that Susannah was pregnant with their first child and Tom begged him to send their fondest love to Ellen.

"Please tell her I'm sorry," he said to Joe, "and ask her to visit us again."

"I will," promised Joe, but still she didn't appear.

At last, one day, John Alderman arrived on their doorstep with good news.

"Sir!" he said. "I'm here to tell you all is well. You've been completely cleared by the Metropolitan police force and judged to be an innocent man. There will never be a stain on your character again."

Tom gasped with relief. "Really?" he said. "And you can marry Ellen?"

"Yes," replied John. "I'm going over to tell her now and start planning our wedding."

"That's wonderful!" exclaimed Phyllis, her eyes shining with joy. "And to think, Tom, now you don't have anything more to fear."

Tom couldn't believe it. At last he could live without fear of his past catching up with him. He felt like a heavy burden had been lifted from his shoulders. He had finally been redeemed. All he had to do now was to reconcile with Ellen.

He needn't have worried. The very next day, Ellen came 'round to see them, flinging her arms around his neck.

"I'm sorry, Father!" she cried. "I was so wrong."

The three of them hugged and cried together, all anger forgotten, a true family again.

The wedding plans went ahead and everyone was very happy. Nevertheless, Tom still wanted to do something to make up for all the distress he had caused Ellen. Maybe he could buy her a present, he thought. Something special. He talked to Phyllis and she agreed it was a good idea, but couldn't think what to suggest.

"Why don't you have a look 'round the local shops?" she said. "There are lots of craftsmen here. Maybe you'll see something."

They scraped together what spare money there was and Tom went out alone. He took his time wandering slowly first around Shoreditch and then the wider area. Eventually, he went into a small shop in Southwark selling glass items made by a local factory and here he found the perfect item.

He visited Ellen the very next Sunday, meeting her after church. He'd already sent a message that he was coming and wanted to take her to tea. She met him happily and they proceeded to a nearby tearoom.

"I wanted to talk to you, Ellen, dear," Tom said. "And I wanted to apologise for all the trouble I've caused you."

"There's no need, Father," she replied. "In fact, you've done me a favour really, because I know now that John loves me more than the police force, and would have married me anyway. But I would like to talk, Father, because I've realised there's a lot I don't know about you and Mother, and your early lives. Please tell me all about it."

So Tom talked at length, telling her of his early life in Devon, the cholera outbreak, his problems with Mary Ann and his dislike of tanning which all led to the one mistake which affected his life from then on. These were all things she didn't know about. He also shocked her by telling her about the conditions in prison and on the hulks, which she had never considered before. It often happens, he thought, that children never realise what their parents have been through. He wondered why it should happen like this, but guessed maybe it was because they were of different generations. In any case, Tom was happy to let her in on his past and to share his memories.

"I'm also grateful to you," Tom said when he had finished. "Because now, finally, I can put my crime behind me and I don't need to feel scared of the law anymore."

"Well, I hope not," laughed Ellen. "You're going to be related to it soon!"

"There's just one more thing," said Tom. "I actually asked you here to give you this, by way of saying sorry. I hope you like it. It seemed the right thing for you."

He handed over the gift which she unwrapped eagerly. It was a small frosted glass bulldog ornament, with jewels for eyes and in its collar. Ellen squealed with delight.

"Oh Father, it's lovely!" she cried. "So beautiful. You know I've always loved dogs. It'll make me think of you every time I look at it. It's so strong and sturdy."

"I wish I was!" laughed Tom. "I feel a bit more on the fragile side these days."

"You've had a hard life, Father," Ellen said. "But you've survived it all. I'm proud to have you for my father!"

Tom couldn't speak for emotion, so they just embraced.

The wedding took place on a golden autumn day in 1885 in the fashionable church of St Georges, in Hanover Square. Ellen looked splendid in a white satin gown, with orange blossom in her dark hair, and John wore his best police uniform. There was even a guard of honour from the local police force to see them out after the ceremony. Tom laughed at the irony of this, but was no longer scared to see so many policemen. He proudly walked Ellen up the aisle and gave her to her future husband. Then he returned to the pew to stand beside his dear wife, Phyllis. Her eyes were shining with emotion, and as he took his place he gave her hand a loving squeeze. She smiled up at him and he whispered in her ear, "I love you!" He was so happy that this day had finally come.

Tom and Phyllis had finally 'retired' now, their various children all contributing to ensure they didn't have to work anymore. They were enjoying a well-deserved time of rest and relaxation at last. As the hymns sounded out, Tom found his mind drifting to reflections on the past.

Ellen was right, he thought, it had been a hard life. There had certainly been some difficult times, he remembered, such as the cholera outbreak, prison and his first marriage break-up. There had been family illnesses and sad losses, such as his little sister Annie, Mary Ann's self-destruction and Fliss' tragic demise. There had also been episodes of great emotional difficulty and distress. However, there had been many good times as well, with people who had believed in him and supported him. He looked around the church and saw most of the people he loved, all there together – sisters, brothers, children, grandchildren. Young Harry, a fine lad of thirteen, stood in the pew next to them. He was working fulltime as an office messenger now, but still living at home as yet. In the pew behind them, Joe, his wife Susannah and their first-born were all there, with another baby due soon. Next to Tom was the person who'd meant more to him than anyone else, who'd been with him through thick and thin, his beloved Phyllis. Her hair was streaked with grey now and there were lines on her face, but she still seemed just as beautiful as ever to him. They'd been married for well over twenty years now and he thanked the Almighty for giving them their time together. Tom knew then, suddenly, that actually his life had been blessed, with the love of his wife, his family and friends. People are all that matter, he decided. If you have the right love and support you can get through anything. Maybe it had been a good life, after all?

The bells rang out as they left the church, Tom holding Phyllis' hand tightly. As they paused outside with the rose petals flying and people cheering the newly weds, he turned to his wife and kissed her passionately, and she responded in equal measure, oblivious to anyone else.

Yes, he thought, *it has been a good life!* and Tom smiled.

Epilogue

Kathleen dusted the ornaments on the shelf, being particularly careful with the glass bulldog. It was a much-treasured possession, given to her by her grandmother Ellen when she was very small. Kathleen's mother was the youngest of Ellen's nine children, all of whom had survived and flourished. She could only just remember her grandmother distantly as a kind old lady who loved dogs, but she had always been fascinated by the bulldog. It was a bit chipped and worn now, and the jewels in its collar had long since disappeared, but she wondered how old it was and what stories it could tell. She could only guess.

NOTE

Since there were no fixed spellings of surnames in the Victorian era, the name Finnimore has been spelt variously over the years (Fennimore, Finnamore, Finamore etc.). To avoid confusion, I have used the original spelling of Finnimore throughout.